A TIME OF FEAR

Book Three of The Time Magnet Series

Russell F. Moran

PREFACE

A Time of Fear is Book Three in *The Time Magnet Series*. *The Gray Ship* is Book One, and *The Thanksgiving Gang* is Book Two.

A Time of Fear picks up where *The Thanksgiving Gang* left off, and joins the gang on their next adventure through time. Like the other two books in *The Time Magnet* series, this is a novel about time travel. Is time travel possible? Theoretically, yes, but I wouldn't try it. What I would try is jumping into this wonderful genre of fiction and lose yourself in the endless possibilities.

This is a work of fiction. Names, characters, businesses, places, events, and incidents are either the products of the author's imagination or used in a fictitious manner. Any resemblance to actual persons, living or dead, or actual events is purely coincidental.

You will see some familiar characters in *A Time of Fear* if you've read the other books. If you haven't, fear not – *A Time of Fear*, although part of a series, can be read as a stand-alone book. Once again you'll meet

Ashley Patterson, the beautiful African American Navy Captain. Jack Thurber is back and he's now Ashley's husband, a man she calls The Time Magnet, because he can't seem to avoid wormholes. Dr. Bennie Weinberg, the NYPD psychiatrist reports for duty, with a much larger role. You will again meet the lovely and feisty Janice Monahan, as well as Wally Burton the reporter from *The New York Times*. Buster, the mega spook CIA Agent and Thanksgiving Gang Leader is here, and he hasn't slowed down. Yes, *the gang*'s all here, and they've really gotten themselves into it this time.

Strange as it may sound, I feel a kinship, a real friendship, with these characters. But my job isn't complete unless you, the reader, feel that you're part of the gang as well.

Once again, as I do in all of my novels, you will see a **Cast of Characters**. Nothing is more annoying than reading a book and trying to remember a character that you met briefly – a couple of hundred pages ago.

So welcome to *the gang*. Join me as, once again, we slip through a wormhole.

ACKNOWLEDGEMENTS

The creative process doesn't exist in a vacuum, but is a result of your experience with life. An ongoing joy of creating fiction is, for me, creating a different world with the help of my wife. After my first draft, Lynda and I spent hours discussing the characters, the scenes, and the story itself. Lynda gave me more than her editorial skills and critiques; she was part of the process, part of the creation. One of the main characters was the result of one of our brain storming sessions.

I also thank my editor and friend, John White for his enthusiasm and dedication to the project.

Characters – A Time of Fear

Abboud, Ayham – Al Qaeda official.

Allheimi, Sheik Abdul – al Qaeda operative, runs a recruiting school.

Akhbar, Gamal – CIA Agent, aka Buster

Billings, John – Navy SEAL lieutenant

Bouchard, Woody – Captain, *The Sea Bounder*

Bradley, Jerome – Shooting victim at CIA

Carlini, William – Director, Central Intelligence Agency

Cropsey, Wayne – Yacht Captain, retired CIA agent

Crowley, Marcus – FBI Agent

Haddad, Abbas – Senior al Qaeda operative

Jefferson, Ezekiel (Zeke) – Commander, aide to Admiral Thompson

Jones, Gordon– Yachtsman

Kabani, Abdul – al Qaeda gunman

Lopez, Phil – Buster's assistant

MacDevitt, Molly – Physics professor and nuclear bomb exert

McMartin, Trevor – Australian bank examiner

Monahan, Janice – HVAC Expert/ Provisional CIA Agent

Monahan, Joseph LCDR – Imprisoned would-be terrorist

Mulrooney, James – NYPD Bomb Disposal Unit

Reynolds, Michael – Professor, Virginia Tech

Thompson, Frank – Rear Admiral, United States Navy

Weinberg, Benjamin – Psychiatrist, NYPD

Williams, Max – Warden, Leavenworth Prison

PROLOGUE

If you think that time travel sounds like fun, I suggest you take up something tamer like skydiving, snake charming, or raising scorpions. Maybe you could catch a ride on top of a moving train or play Russian Roulette with an AK-47. Perhaps you could walk into a radical mosque, loudly reciting the Hail Mary.

There are a lot of things that you could do that are safer than time travel. Other things may be safer, but sometimes time travel is useful.

My name is Jack Thurber, and everybody knows me as a time traveler. I've done it four times to date. My wife Ashley even calls me a "time magnet." I don't time travel intentionally; nobody does. It just happens. Step on a wormhole and you're in for a wild ride, a sickening, weird ride.

Avoid wormholes. How? I'm not sure I'm the guy to tell you because I sure can't seem to avoid the damn things.

Right now I'm relaxed and happy and living in the present. It's October 18, 2015, and I'm with the woman I love, my wife Ashley. Until recently we thought we were dead. How can you *think* you're dead when you're alive? I'll explain. Well, I'll try to explain.

About four months ago on July 1, 2015, I was on assignment as a reporter for the *Washington Times*, on location in Manhattan to do research for an article I was writing on underutilized real estate. Exciting? No, but soon it became a thrill that I wasn't looking for. As I walked through an abandoned lot I stepped on, you guessed it, a wormhole. Like a flash, and it really was like a flash, I was standing there in the lot on July 1, 2017, two years into the future. I didn't plan it, didn't think about it, didn't try to make it happen. The future just showed up, and I was in it.

Confused, as I always was on one of my time trips, I called my old friend Bennie Weinberg, a psychiatrist and detective with the NYPD. Bennie knew about my time-tripping proclivities, but he treated me like some kind of an apparition, a freak, a ghost. It seemed that, according to Ben, I had been killed about two years prior to arriving in 2017, along with my wife Ashley and about 26,000 people on five different aircraft carriers in a series of nuclear terrorist attacks. That's right, according to Ben, Ashley and I were blown to bits on November 26, 2015. Ashley was the commanding officer of one of the ships and I was aboard as her guest for a Thanksgiving Cruise.

Bennie and I teamed up with my friend Wally Burton, a reporter with *The New York Times*, and a woman named Janice Monahan, the wife of one of the terrorists. We called ourselves The Thanksgiving Gang, and proceeded to go back in time (thank God I remembered where the wormhole was) and prevented the disaster.

It worked. With help from the FBI, the CIA, and a lot of other agencies, it worked. I'm here, Ashley's here, and we're both alive and in love.

My good friends and fellow "gang" members, Ben, Janice, and Wally decided to go back (back?) to 2017 where they came from. They left for the future on October 18, 2015.

So that clears it all up, yes? No? Wait. It gets weirder.

CHAPTER ONE

Something's wrong.

Something's terribly wrong.

This isn't the way it's supposed to be.

My name is Janice Monahan, and I'm scared out of my mind. I just went through a wormhole (or time portal) along with my friends Wally Burton and Ben Weinberg. We came from October 18, 2015 and arrived in October 18, 2017. I realize that sounds insane, and I would agree that it is, but it's also true. The three of us just time tripped two years into the future.

I'm living an exciting life, and I owe it all to my terrorist, would-be mass murdering husband. More about him later. Until about a month ago I was a diligent HVAC engineer working on a major project and minding my own business. I had no idea where my husband was, nor did I care. I had fallen out of love with the man, a man who I didn't know anymore, a man who turned his back on me and his country.

It was only three weeks ago that I answered the doorbell at my house in Brooklyn. Three guys, Jack Thurber, Ben Weinberg, and Wally Burton appeared at my door. They gave me a story that they were reporters from *The New York Times* and were writing a magazine article on the impact of what we knew as the Thanksgiving Attacks, nuclear attacks on five American ships. Actually, Wally Burton really *is* a reporter with the *Times*. They wanted to interview me because I was the widow of Joseph Monahan, an officer on one of the ships. What they didn't know, and what I didn't know at the time, was that my husband was one of the murderous bastards who conspired to bomb the ships. Their ruse about writing an article was just that, a ruse. Jack Thurber and his friends were trying to find out everything they could about the attacks. It seemed that Jack Thurber, in our "then history" of 2017, was known to be dead. He was killed, along with his Navy captain wife, on one of the ships, the one my charming husband was supposed to be on. Jack convinced Ben and Wally, and eventually me, that he actually travelled two years through time, skipping over the attacks on the ships and avoiding his death. Jack wanted to go back to 2015 and prevent the disaster. Who could blame him? He believed he had the power to undo a tragedy, his death and that of his wife. After many discussions and meetings that included the FBI and CIA, we all decided to go back in time with Jack to help him prevent the attacks.

Along with Jack, we dubbed ourselves the *Thanksgiving Gang*, a collective *Mighty Mouse* that would save the day and avert a big disaster on Thanksgiving Day 2015.

We pulled it off. The Thanksgiving Gang, along with the FBI and the CIA, stopped the attacks on the five carriers and saved about 26,000 people, including Jack and his wife Ashley. We all thought we'd live happily ever after. Nice thought. Or was it a dream?

━◈ ◈━

As I stepped on the wormhole, I felt like I was plunged into ice water. Ben and Wally agreed with my assessment. The temperature was fine, a typical late October day, about 60 degrees, bright and sunny. But we may as well have landed on the surface of Mars.

We expected to arrive at a construction site on 1st Avenue and 118th Street in Manhattan. It appeared somewhat familiar, until we looked south. Instead of the endless view of monumental skyscrapers, there was rubble, except for some buildings a few blocks from us. In large part, lower Manhattan had been destroyed. I looked up at a strange instrument on a telephone pole. It was marked "radiation meter." It indicated that we were in a place of low to moderate radiation. We guessed that what happened to lower Manhattan was a nuclear explosion.

We expected to arrive in a different 2017, a happier 2017, a year that didn't have a history of five aircraft carriers destroyed two years before. The Thanksgiving Gang had saved the day. But what were the carrier attacks replaced with?

CHAPTER TWO

I feel like I'm going to throw up. The three of us concluded that a nuclear attack happened in Manhattan and God knows where else. We all figured that it was a nuclear attack because of the devastation. The radiation meter on the pole seemed to confirm our conclusion.

When the gang tripped back the last time we found that time in the past goes faster than the present. Don't ask; it just does. Three weeks of 2017 time amounted to three months in 2015. Oh my God. In a matter of weeks (2015 weeks that is) Manhattan will become a nuclear target. From our view, in 2017, it already had.

Ben, Wally, and I went to Wally's office at *The New York Times* on Eighth Avenue. We needed to find out exactly what happened, and figured what better place to get information. Because we had discovered that time goes by faster in the past, our recent journey to 2015 was only a matter of a couple of hours in 2017.

"Long lunch?" asked Gloria, Wally's secretary. From her perspective, she hadn't seen Wally for two hours.

Wally introduced us and then told Gloria that he was planning a long article about the Thanksgiving Day attacks. "You and every other reporter in the world," said Gloria.

Wally asked her if she could save him some time by finding a video about the event. Obviously he didn't want her to think that we didn't know anything about the disaster.

"Here," she said, reaching into a cabinet for a CD. "This documentary is probably the best. It covers everything in three hours."

Wally inserted the first disc into his computer, and we began to watch the scariest horror movie we'd ever seen. It was a collaboration of CNN, CBS, and Fox News. At the beginning, the narrator explained that so many reporters lost their lives in the attacks that they had to pool some journalistic talent. The film was produced by Steven Spielberg and narrated by James Earl Jones and Al Pacino.

"Each of the bombs, as we now know," said James Earl Jones, "was a suitcase nuke, each about 10-kilotons. By way of comparison, the bomb that was dropped on Hiroshima was between 12 and 18-kilotons. Part of what we know came from the bombs that were confiscated from the Detroit factory, the ones that were supposed to be used on the five aircraft carriers. Well, that plot was broken by a group of people who called themselves the Thanksgiving Gang."

We all looked at each other and smiled.

"From what we understand," said Jones, "there was a lot of rejoicing, back slapping, and high- fiving from that Thanksgiving Gang as well as the CIA, the FBI, and the Office of Naval Intelligence. A horrible attack was avoided. There was some concern that Ayham Abboud, the al Qaeda leader who was in charge of the operation, escaped. The thinking was, at all levels of government, that he would eventually be captured, just like Osama bin Laden. Everybody sat down to Thanksgiving dinner that day with something to be thankful for. But at the same time the ships were supposed to be hit, at 3 PM Eastern Time, America had its heart ripped out."

"Before the attacks," Jones continued, "numerous engineering studies predicted the result of different size nuclear blasts in various American cities. But the studies underestimated the impact of a nuclear blast in a city of skyscrapers. What we now know is that every piece of metal or cement that wasn't vaporized became part of a high-speed cloud of flying projectiles, taking down building after building in its path. That's why lower Manhattan was devastated."

As he spoke, aerial views of the crumbled cities appeared on the screen.

"I'm now going to give you the results," Jones said, "city by city."

"The first is Chicago. The bomb was detonated next to the Willis Tower, once known as the Sears Tower, the eleventh tallest building in the world. It now seems obvious to us that one of the terrorists' objectives was to destroy American icons. You'll see what I mean as we look at the other cities. The death toll in Chicago, which keeps climbing as people succumb to radiation sickness and develop cancers, is just over 200,000. The number was kept down because the attack happened on a holiday in a business district. About a quarter-mile radius from the Willis Tower is total devastation, and other large buildings were destroyed as far as three-quarters of a mile away, with major damage for a mile around. It would take hours to list the areas that were destroyed so I won't. Just know that LaSalle Street, the Daley Center, Roosevelt University, the Chicago Art Institute, almost all of South Wacker Drive – they're all history."

The film was nauseating. I've spent a lot of time in Chicago on various projects, and always enjoyed taking long walks through the city. I loved the architecture in Chicago. On the screen in front of me, instead of beautiful buildings, there was rubble as far as the eye could see.

He then turned to Los Angeles.

"Los Angeles didn't suffer the enormous devastation that Chicago and New York experienced, only because there weren't as many tall buildings near the detonation point. But parts of the city were clearly destroyed, including the iconic Hollywood sign. People have speculated about Hollywood as a target because the attackers wanted to strike at the heart of a unique American institution."

Al Pacino narrated the attack on New York.

"After two attempts on the World Trade Center, one in 1993 and the plane attacks of 9/11, the terrorists apparently wanted to destroy the site once and for all. The blast, because of all the surrounding tall buildings, took out much more of the city than anybody would expect of a 10- kiloton bomb. Just as in Chicago, the materials from the buildings were turned into a fire storm of flying debris. Wall Street is now a vacant lot. The municipal buildings, including City Hall and the court buildings were damaged beyond repair."

As he spoke, the film showed the names of the destroyed buildings on a graphic overlay. Federal Hall on Wall Street, the site of George Washington's inauguration, was rubble. These bastards wanted to destroy our history. That's me talking, not Pacino.

I'd seen enough. From the introduction at the beginning of the narration, I knew that the Golden Gate Bridge in San Francisco was destroyed, as well as the Washington Monument and the Capital Building in Washington, D.C. The White House sustained heavy damage. Because of the Thanksgiving holiday, only 50 Congressmen and 12 Senators were killed. The President and First Lady were at Fort Bragg, North Carolina, celebrating the day with the troops of the 82nd Airborne Division.

"We gotta go," I said to Ben and Wally. "Today's October 18, only six weeks to Thanksgiving Day."

"Go where?" they both asked.

"We've got to go back to the wormhole," I said. "We know that today is October 18. We know that time goes faster in the past than in the present, and from that movie we just saw as well as our own eyes, we know what will happen in less than two months. And most important, we know where the wormhole is. We've got to go back to stop these attacks just like we went back to stop the attacks on the ships. I don't think there's anything to talk about. We gotta do it."

We talked about the timing of our return to 2015. I wanted to go back immediately, but Ben and Wally had concerns.

"I'm staying here for a bit longer," said Wally. "I want to bring as much information back with me as possible."

"Me too," said Ben. "I want to talk to my people at the NYPD and find out more. We want as much information as we can get our hands on before we go time-tripping back."

"Well, I'm going back NOW," I said. "Somebody's got to blow the whistle and put things in motion."

Both Ben and Wally agreed that I should go back as soon as possible. They said they'd follow me the next day.

As I walked to the wormhole site I wondered how the hell we could do anything in six weeks. We had a lot of time before the ship attacks were supposed to happen, and we had a lot of research to start with, not to mention Wally Burton's brilliant investigative reporting. Now we've got squat, other than the CD video "evidence" in my shoulder bag. I won't have a hard time convincing my time travel friends on the other side of the wormhole, but what do we do then? I've just got to get back and sweat the details later.

I approached the lot where the wormhole was located, getting ready for my third time trip in a matter of weeks. This is nuts. I'm hoping to wake up and find that this has been a strange dream.

As I walked up to the grate a man called my name.

CHAPTER THREE

"Mrs. Monahan, shouted the man as he approached me. "May I have a word with you?"

Shit, what a time to be without my Glock. I'm a deadly accurate shot, but that talent doesn't work without a gun. The guy didn't seem menacing, but with all the crazy crap I've been through recently I wasn't about to let my guard down. Beside my skill with a pistol, one of my favorite workout routines is kick boxing. As the man got near me I visualized my right foot crushing his nuts.

"Please, Madam, I just need to speak with you. Where are your friends?"

"To what friends are you referring," I asked, "and who the hell are you?"

The guy was quite tall and handsome. He looked Middle Eastern, but wore no beard, sported khaki pants and a navy blue blazer. A preppy wouldn't be a mugger now would he?

"My name is Ayham Abboud."

"Ayham Abboud," I shouted, as I readied my right leg and foot. "Any relation to an al Qaeda big shot with the same name?"

"I am not the Ayham Abboud who you think I am."

"Well how about a straight answer to a simple fucking question?" I inquired pleasantly. "Are you him or not?"

"Appearances are not what they appear to be, Madam."

The guy didn't look or sound at all threatening. But what the hell do I know. I'm the woman who married a man committed to mass murder. I wish Bennie Weinberg was here. Bennie's a shrink with the NYPD and can smell bullshit a mile away.

"Are you armed?" I said, trying not to show my fear.

"Yes, Madam," he said as he casually reached into his pocket, took out a nine-millimeter pistol, and gave it to me, handle forward. He did this before my talented right foot was about to connect with his crotch.

"Now *you* are in charge of this conversation," he said. "I am well aware of your talents with a pistol."

CHAPTER FOUR

"Okay, so let me get this straight," I said, "you're a terrorist who hands me a gun, knowing that I can blow your head off."

"Yes, Madam, and I also know of your bravery and that you wouldn't hesitate to shoot me."

This conversation was starting to suffer from a lack of direction. A killer gives me his gun and chats like we're feeding pigeons in the park.

"What do you want?" I said. If he gives me some more poetic crap like when I asked his identity, maybe I *will* shoot him.

"I know that you're about to go through the wormhole, it's right there," he said pointing to the portal. "I knew you would be here eventually. I've been waiting for you for quite some time."

"Okay, pal, as I expected you didn't answer my fucking question, so I'll repeat it. What do you want?"

I've noticed that when I'm frightened my language gets vulgar. Maybe I should kick this guy in the nuts. I'll feel better, and I'll speak more ladylike.

"I wish to accompany you back to the year 2015, through the portal," he said, nodding to the wormhole. "I can go alone or accompany you. Believe me, Madam, it is best that we went together."

"Alright," I said, "here's another simple question – why?"

"I want to help you stop the Thanksgiving Attacks. I'm the only one who can."

CHAPTER FIVE

My elusive Arab conversationalist finally made a point, a good point, actually a winning point. I've got a gun and a quick right foot. How risky can this be? I'm dying to continue this conversation – on the other side of the wormhole.

We walked up to the metal grate. My stomach was in a knot, as I expected.

"Have you ever done this before?" I asked.

"In my life I have done many things, Madam."

Here he goes again. Whatever else he's done in his life, answering questions doesn't appear to be one of them.

"Okay, here's the drill. I'll go first and you follow behind me."

No way would I step through the portal with Omar here waiting for me on the other side.

I stepped through the wormhole, felt the normal dizziness and slight nausea, immediately took the safety off my new-found pistol, and turned to meet him. He appeared, took one step, and fell onto his side shaking his head. He tried to stand up and barfed. If this man's a time traveler he's out of practice. I held his arm as we walked over to a nearby vendor. My girl scout days came back to me, and I felt kind of bad for the guy. I wanted to get him some water so he could rinse his mouth out. I also reached into my purse and handed him a small bottle of mouthwash.

"Are you okay?" I asked him, suddenly concerned for his safety. He nodded and smiled sheepishly as I handed him a wad of cleansing towlettes. Even though I just saw my Arab friend throw up, I was starving, so I figured we'd have a quick meal at a nearby food cart. I asked him if he could use something to eat since he just lost his breakfast. He nodded. I expected him to order falafel or some shit, but instead he asked for a hot dog with extra sauerkraut. Getting to know this guy will be a work in progress.

Norfolk, Virginia, our destination, is about 350 miles from here, or six hours driving time, which should get us there around 5 PM. I didn't want to fly because it would be impossible to get the gun through security, and the gun was *my* security. I also figured he could tell me his story on the way, and probably evade every goddam question I ask him.

"Do you know how to drive a car, Mr. Abboud?"

"Life has many pleasures, Madam, and driving a motor vehicle is one of them."

"That's a lovely observation," I said, "but at the risk of repeating myself, *can you drive a fucking car?*"

"Yes, Madam."

It's going to be a long six hours, I thought. We got to the car rental place and I picked out a Ford Explorer. I didn't ask him what he wanted, because I didn't care. He was the hitchhiker after all.

I made sure we got a car with a GPS because holding a gun and fumbling with maps don't go together.

I told him to get into the car while I made a phone call. I had to get in touch with Jack and Ashley to let them know that I came back through the wormhole and that I'm (we're) coming. I quickly explained to Jack that I had some horrible news which I'd share when we met in Norfolk. I also told Jack about my road trip buddy who calls himself Ayham Abboud. I thought Jack would freak out on me. I told him about Abboud giving me his gun, and that he'd be driving. Jack knows I can handle a gun and that seemed to calm him down. We agreed to meet at the Marriott in Norfolk. I told him that Ben and Wally would be heading back to 2015 the next day.

I wish I could say that I'm getting used to this insanity, but I'm not.

CHAPTER SIX

After I got off the phone with Jack I leaned against the car and pretended to make another call. I was buying time to get my thoughts together. It occurred that I was about to take a 350-mile trip with a guy who's a known terrorist, probably a mass murderer. But he seemed, and this may sound stupid, like a nice guy, almost pleasant. He was polite, even courtly, the way he called me "madam." What I knew about him, or what I thought I knew about him, wasn't lining up with my actual experience of him. I needed to know some more about this man before our road trip. I got into the passenger seat of the car, with the pistol in my lap. As he was about to turn on the ignition, I told him to wait.

"I can't go any further until I know some more about you," I said. "Are you the man who engineered the nuclear attacks on the five American aircraft carriers? We know the attacks didn't happen, but are you the mastermind or not?"

"I realize that you're impatient with me when I don't answer your questions directly, Madam, but I believe it would be best for me to disclose everything in the company of your friends, the ones you call The Thanksgiving Gang, as well as the proper authorities."

"Just a damn minute," I said. "We know what happened on Thanksgiving Day, 2015. We just came from the year 2017 and saw the devastation. Instead of the ships, five American cities were nuked. Now here we are, back in 2015, just weeks before the attacks. You have to answer this question – Were you in charge of that operation as well?"

"The simple answer, Madam, and it *will* be a simple answer, is NO. Absolutely not. But we both know that these attacks will happen, and that's what I want to prevent. If I have to sacrifice my own life to stop the bombs, I shall happily do so."

"Thanks for answering a question for a change," I said, "but I have a follow-up. Did you or did you not act as mentor and spiritual advisor to the bomb planting naval officers when they were only teenagers on a trip to Saudi Arabia? Did you not convert them to Islam and engage them in the conspiracy to nuke the American ships?"

"I will also answer that question, Madam. Yes, in 1994 I took these kids, who were on a school trip, and converted them to Islam. I can be persuasive, especially with young people. I not only converted them to Islam but to radical Islam, to a life of hatred of all things Western, a double life of jihadists and American naval officers."

"Then exactly why should I trust you?"

"Because, Madam, I am not *that* man. Yes, I am Ayham Abboud, but not the Abboud who you feared and hated. I shall disclose my life to you and your friends and to anyone who asks. I just request that we wait until we get to Norfolk."

I felt like a thirsty cat that was just given a spoon full of milk. I wanted more, but he wanted to hold his fire until we all get together. I'm sitting next to a man who is a known terrorist, but he says he's not, even though he bears the name Ayham Abboud. But he wants to wait till we get to Norfolk to talk. What choice do I have? I'm not going to shoot the guy. At least I don't think so.

We were approaching the Vince Lombardi Service area on the New Jersey Turnpike when Abboud said, "Madam, I'm going to pull off at the next rest stop to attend to matters."

"You can attend to matters," I said. "I'll pee."

When Abboud pulled into a parking spot and turned off the car, I was reaching down to pick up my bag. In an instant he walked around the car and opened the door for me. After he opened the door he gestured with his hand for me to step out. This is not going easy on my head. He's not only pleasant to be with, he's an old fashioned gentleman. He's also quite good looking. Stop right there girl! I reminded myself that my husband Joe Monahan was a handsome and charming guy who was prepared to murder thousands of people. Didn't I read somewhere that Osama bin Laden was a gentlemanly sort?

I turned my back to a group of people to conceal what I was about to do. "Look at this," I said, as I put the safety switch on the pistol and placed the gun in my bag. He showed good faith by giving me his gun, so I figured I would show him some return good faith. It's always a more pleasant experience to travel with someone who isn't able to kill you in an instant.

We "attended to matters" and met near the rest stop exit. Abboud offered to stand in line to get us a couple of sodas. I noticed that he was wearing dark sunglasses and had a Yankees cap pulled down over his forehead. I stood there observing the travelers coming and going. These people don't know who this guy is. They have no idea that he planned the deaths of a few thousand people and trained five young boys for a life of murder. They don't know this man.

Do I?

We got back into the car and started to leave the parking lot. As we came to a traffic aisle, a car driven by a teenager suddenly shot right in front of us, forcing Abboud to hit the brakes and me to spit my Diet Coke all over the dashboard. The kid turned and flipped us the universal sign of disapproval. I expected Abboud to curse and pound the steering wheel. Instead, he bowed his head slightly and put his hands together in a prayerful gesture, as if to telegraph to the brat "I'm sorry." This guy has a control over his emotions that you don't often see. I could use some of that myself.

I wiped the soda from the dashboard and myself and glanced at my car buddy. I'm sitting next to a man who is a complete mystery. He's definitely an easy travelling companion, and our pleasant chatting has calmed the knot in my stomach. I decided that it was about time to talk like a couple of friendly acquaintances, and maybe lift the mood a bit.

"We have about 125 miles to go," I said. "What should I call you? I've been calling you Mr. Abboud – I refuse to call you Sheik. You can call me Janice. I hate the name Mrs. Monahan."

"Please call me Frank, Janice."

"Frank? Fucking Frank?" I inquired in my ladylike way.

"No, Janice, just Frank."

CHAPTER SEVEN

Even though we were now on a first name basis, (I still can't get that the guy's name is so simple and American) the conversation continued to be stilted because Frankie of Arabia wanted to hold up on his story till we got to Norfolk. So I clicked onto an audio book site on my iPhone. I read through a few titles when Frank requested that we listen to *Things that Matter* by Charles Krauthammer, a book consisting of the author's writings over the past couple of decades. It's a book I've been meaning to read or listen to so I agreed with his selection.

"But Krauthammer's a conservative writer and pundit, and an American patriot," I said. "I don't know why but I'm surprised you'd want to listen to him."

"He's a brilliant intellectual and historian, Janice. He's also an admirable man who's a quadriplegic as a result of a youthful swimming accident. He knows how to overcome adversity. Krauthammer's one of my favorite people."

I didn't think Sheik Frankie was what the Republican establishment thinks of as part of "the base." But then as the time and miles go by, I'm not sure what anybody can think of my road trip buddy. I sure as hell don't know what to think of him. But I can't believe I'm actually starting to like him.

I have to admit that my mind kept wandering from the words of Dr. Krauthammer, much as I enjoy him. I kept taking glances at my road companion, Frank. He really is handsome and has a slender athletic build. Okay, stop right there girl. I reminded myself that less than a month ago I was a quiet engineer working on a heating and air conditioning plant for a bank in New Jersey. In the last few weeks I discovered that my husband was a terrorist and potential mass murderer. Now I'm sitting here next to a man named Ayham Abboud who calls himself Frank. I know that he is (was?) a serious terrorist who held a key to the executive men's room at al Qaeda, Inc. I know (I think I know) that he was the prime mover in the attempted destruction of five American warships. And I'm getting to like him. Maybe I should apply for a spot on a reality TV show.

I ponder this fact. Captain Patterson calls her husband Jack a "Time Magnet" because he has a habit of stepping on wormholes. Maybe I'm a "Jihadi Magnet." I seem to attract them, no? First Joe, now Frank. No matter how good looking this guy is, I'm cooling it until further notice. Also in the last few weeks I thought I was falling in love with Jack Thurber until I found out that his wife Ashley was still alive. I realized that it would never happen between me and Jack. So now Frankie of Arabia is looking good to me. Is he just a rebound from Jack, and was Jack just a rebound from my treasonous husband? I think I mentioned before that I'm confused.

It hasn't gotten any better.

CHAPTER EIGHT

The strangest road trip in my life was coming to an end. I had just gotten a call from Jack telling me that our meeting location had been changed to CIA headquarters at Langley, Virginia. It's about 25 miles north of Norfolk so it shaved some time off our trip. Jack wouldn't say why we were meeting at the CIA.

We drove up to the gate and gave our names to the guard. I told the guard that I was armed and, as I expected, he asked for my (Frank's) gun and temporarily confiscated it.

It was obvious that they expected us because a Marine guard escorted us from our car to the headquarters building. It's a well-designed structure with a curved entranceway covered by glass skylights. As we walked to the entrance I kept thinking that I was an HVAC engineer and consultant, and here I was going to a meeting at the Central Intelligence Agency. I'd been to the CIA before, about three weeks before, in what now seemed like another lifetime. Back then we were The Thanksgiving Gang, working to stop the attacks on the carriers. Who am I now, and what am I doing here?

Once inside the building our Marine escort passed us off to a guy in a business suit. We took the elevator and were then escorted into the office of William Carlini, Director of the CIA. I didn't expect this. It's clear that some important people are interested in me and my travelling companion.

We were led to a conference room next to Carlini's office. A couple of minutes after Frank and I walked in, Ben and Wally appeared. I introduced Frank as...well, Frank. I told them he would fill us in on his role shortly. I hoped they were looking forward to his explanation as much as I was. I wondered why Ben and Wally were already there, and Wally explained that they had decided that additional research would slow down the operation, so they hopped a plane from JFK.

Also at the meeting would be Captain Ashley Patterson, Jack Thurber, and CIA Director Carlini.

As soon as Ashley and Jack walked in, Ashley yelled, "Admiral Thompson, so great to see you, Frank." They hugged as old friends.

"Admiral?" I screamed, embarrassing myself as usual. "You're a fucking admiral?"

"Actually, Janice, I'm a *rear* admiral," said Frankie of Arabia with a smile. Director Carlini cracked up at my dainty choice of words.

I wasn't the only one in shock. Jack, Ben, and Wally stood there with their mouths open.

"But Janice told me that she was with Ayham Abboud," said Jack. "What is it, are you a naval officer or an al Qaeda jihadist?"

"Folks, let me explain," said Carlini. "Frank Thompson is definitely a naval officer and a good one. They don't make people admirals unless they're qualified. What I'm about to say is Top Secret. As you folks recall, I swore you in as provisional CIA Agents during our hunt for the would-be ship attackers. I'm now officially renewing that status. You are all provisional agents of the CIA and you're expected to follow precise security protocols. Please take your seats while I explain."

We sat around the long conference table and faced Carlini, who sat at the head in the command position.

"Besides being a Navy Admiral," Carlini continued, "Frank Thompson has acted for the last 20 years as the deepest mole in American history. Yes, his other name is Ayham Abboud, a leader of al Qaeda and sworn enemy of the United States. He's known in the ranks of terrorists as Sheik Ayham Abboud, a feared and cunning operative. He's also an Oscar caliber actor. I don't know how he does it. I'm going to ask Frank to fill you in on what he's been up to, and most importantly, how we're going to stop the nuclear attacks on five American cities that are scheduled to happen just a few weeks from now."

"Pardon me, Mr. Director," I said. "How could you possibly know that? All I told Jack on the phone was that I had some horrible information to share, information that I learned in 2017. I didn't tell Jack what happened. Has someone else travelled through the wormhole?"

"I think Frank will clear this up for all of you," said Carlini.

Frank moved to the opposite head of the table. He is definitely one good looking man. He carries himself like an athlete and stands before people like a born leader.

"Except for Janice and Director Carlini, you folks are in the dark, so I'm now going to enlighten you. On Thanksgiving Day, less than six weeks from now, al Qaeda will launch five nuclear attacks on American cities. The Thanksgiving Attacks on American aircraft carriers were stopped, as you all know, and you had a lot to do with preventing the disaster. What will soon replace those attacks will be far worse. But it won't happen. We're going to stop them. The Thanksgiving Gang isn't ready to retire."

"Excuse me," I said, "but I need to get something clear in my head, something about you. Are you not the Ayham Abboud who masterminded the Thanksgiving Attacks on the ships? If it wasn't for us and the CIA and FBI those attacks would have happened. I personally saw drone surveillance videos of you, or somebody who looked like you, going into that bomb factory in Detroit. We stopped you didn't we? Well, didn't we?"

"I was going to get to that," said Frank, "but I think it's a good idea to clear this up for all of you now. While I admire the excellent work that everyone did, how do you think a drone surveillance project could have uncovered the plot so quickly? The answer is that I, as well as Director Carlini, knew exactly what was happening. Hell, Abboud, that's me, was the guy who was making it happen. Who do you think leaked the Arabic names of the Atomic Five to the newspapers? Also, did you see the reports from the SEALs that mentioned that the men guarding the bombs appeared sluggish? That's because I drugged them on my last visit."

"Frank," Ashley said. "I've known you for as long as I've been in the Navy. We once served together on the *Independence* when you were her commanding officer. You also commanded a Carrier Strike Group in the Persian Gulf. Where did you find the time to play James Bond?"

"Yes, Ashley," said Frank, "I'm definitely a blue water sailor like yourself. But a large part of my life has been under deep cover."

"How long in advance did you start this operation?" asked Jack.

"About 20 years ago," said Frank.

"What?" we all said simultaneously.

"I was a 23-year-old Navy lieutenant in 1993, just two years out of Annapolis. While I was stationed on a destroyer, we discovered a bomb plot. The captain contacted the Office of Naval Intelligence and they jumped in. I helped them every step of the way because I was the ship's weapons officer and they suspected the plot may have hatched inside my department. We found the man who planned the bombing, a disgruntled chief petty officer. He's still in prison. The officer who handled the operation for the Office of Naval Intelligence took a liking to me, and gave the captain a glowing report, which said they couldn't have done it without me. Over beers, the guy told me I should consider a career in naval intelligence, given my flair for investigation. I didn't want to give up my career as a sea-going officer, but he did convince me that naval intelligence could be part of my portfolio. About a year later I learned that the Navy had some big plans for me. Working closely with the head of the CIA at the time, the Navy hatched a long term plan to test our vulnerability to a suit-case nuclear attack. I'd like to think they picked me for my brilliance, but a lot of the decision-making had to do with my looks. I appear Middle Eastern, as you can see, a trait inherited from my Lebanese mother."

"Frank," said Carlini, "please tell them about your training and how you wound up in Saudi Arabia."

"As part of my training I was sent for intensive study of Arabic. I was always pretty good at languages so I picked it up fast. The CIA – by the way these guys are brilliant – came up with a plan for me to "defect," and volunteer to help al Qaeda to find susceptible young Americans to act as operatives, a nice word for "home grown terrorists." With the help of a few select CIA moles I was soon con-tacted by a man known as Sheik Abdul Allheimi. He told me that he had heard (from the moles of course) that I was interested in the cause of Islam. This man ran a program in Riyadh known as *The Center for Open-Minded Youth,* which was a recruiting tool funded by Saudi Arabia. Each summer they would host groups of American and European teenagers on a trip to Riyadh. Their overall objective was to nurture home grown jihadis. Allheimi wanted me to act as mentor to a group of selected American kids, to gain their trust to convert them to Islam. He wanted me for the job because I was a native American, and, because I was in my early-20s, I could relate to high school seniors."

"Was one of these boys a kid known as Joseph Monahan?" I asked.

"Yes, Janice, one of them was your future husband."

"Who is now rotting in prison," I said. "I'm sorry, I know that's totally irrelevant. I just enjoy hearing myself say it." (I really have to work on my anger issues about Joseph Monahan.)

"So I took these impressionable boys under my wing. The Navy wanted me to use these kids in the plot to attack the American ships. When the time was appropriate, I would discuss the plans with my al Qaeda contacts. I encouraged the kids, as they grew into adulthood, to become naval officers, an essential part of the plot. The rest, as we know, is history. The Atomic Five, as you call them, were arrested and are now in prison as a result of operation Tango Delta, thanks in no small part to you folks."

So did my road trip pal, this charming admiral, destroy the lives of five kids? I'm having a hard time with the ethics of this operation. If he never met them, none of them would be a part of the Atomic Five, because there never would have been a Thanksgiving Attack operation. I've got to clear this up, I decided, if only in my own head.

"Frank," I said, "does your conscience give you any problems knowing the path you set these kids on? I mean, if they never knew you they wouldn't be in prison right now."

"Janice, that's not only a key question, it's the most important question of my life. The answer is 'no,' but it's not a simple no. *The Center for Open-Minded Youth* is an ongoing operation aimed at turning American youth to jihad. The Navy used me to create this complicated operation to check on our vulnerabilities, and to use the kids to do so. These five kids would have become faceless suicide bombers somewhere in the world. I simply focused them in a direction that would help the United States."

I felt much better. He was right. If not him it would have been another American, and the path these kids took would have been much worse, and they probably would have all died. I also couldn't help but notice how straight-forward, intelligent, and handsome the guy was. He has a commanding voice, lots of brains, and a solid character. From what he said about school and his age, he's in his early to mid-forties. I decided it was time to do a little investigation myself.

"You must have driven your wife crazy with the double life you've led for twenty years," I said. I saw Bennie start to laugh and then put his face into his hands. Bennie knows me better than I know myself sometimes.

"I lost my wife, Alice, to cancer ten years ago. Since then I've been married to my work."

"I'm sorry for your loss, Frank." I said.

Interesting. Frank's in his mid-forties, handsome, brilliant, and single.

I'm feeling much better.

CHAPTER NINE

"I'll take it from here, Frank," said Carlini. "When your Australian friend, the bank examiner Trevor McMartin, was kidnapped and presumably assassinated in 2017 we knew we had a problem, that al Qaeda was on to us. McMartin gave you folks some great leads and information, and we weren't the only ones who knew that. Somehow his cover got blown."

"Excuse me," said Jack, "as you said, that was in 2017 – on the other side of the wormhole. How can you possibly know about the murder of Trevor McMartin?"

"Frank?" said Carlini, nodding to the admiral.

"You folks aren't the only ones who travelled through the wormhole. Why did you think I was waiting there for you, Janice?"

Maybe you just wanted to meet a nice looking lady, I thought. *Oh stop this crap now.*

"So we realized that we had a problem, a big one," continued Carlini. "I immediately took Frank out of circulation. Al Qaeda doesn't know what happened to him. His job has been replaced by a man known as Sheik Abbas Haddad. He's the one who tried to pull the trigger on the Thanksgiving Attacks. As we know, Haddad escaped."

"Are we sure al Qaeda doesn't know anything about Frank other than that he's missing?" I asked, suddenly concerned about the safety of my road-trip buddy.

"Frank is in the shadows, Janice," said Carlini, "except for his car ride with you."

"I guess that explains the hat and sunglasses every time we stopped," I said.

Frank just looked at me and winked. I was about to wink back when he turned his head toward Carlini.

"Here's our problem," said Carlini, "and yes, I've alerted the White House. We had absolutely no knowledge of their Plan B, the attacks on the American cities. Not only that, but we had no knowledge of the existence of the other five bombs. Frank didn't know about them, and if Frank didn't know, nobody else in our government knew. This is the most secretive operation al Qaeda has ever launched. Even 9/11, in retrospect, had some warning signs. The signs were ignored, as we all know, but they were there. Now, we've had no hints about this plot at all. If it weren't for that wonderful wormhole, we'd all be drifting ignorantly toward disaster."

"But here's the worst part," said Carlini, "we don't know where the other bombs are."

"But we may have a secret weapon of our own," Admiral Frank chimed in.

CHAPTER TEN

After Frank mentioned the "secret weapon," both he and Carlini looked at me. Oh shit, I thought, I knew where this was going. They were planning a reunion between me and my son-of-a-bitch husband.

"Why are you two looking at me?" I asked, as if I didn't know.

"We want you to visit your husband at Leavenworth," said Carlini. "That's the simple answer to your question. It's not an easy answer, but it's a simple answer."

"Would it be impolite, sir, if I throw up on the conference table?" I asked.

Carlini chuckled at my impudent wisecrack. "I told you the answer wasn't easy, just simple. We've huddled with some of our top forensic psychiatric people, and they're the ones who led me to this plan. I'm going to ask Dr. Ben over here to listen carefully to what I'm about to say, and to please correct me if he thinks I'm wrong."

I once had a dream that I was walking toward the edge of a cliff. I wanted to stop, but my legs kept walking. I grabbed at tree branches to slow my progress, but my legs continued on. That's how I felt as Carlini spoke.

"According to our shrinks, Joseph Monahan is second guessing his actions right now. He's been in solitary since he was arrested and has no communication with anyone. Our psychiatrist friends think that you may be only one in the world who may be able to get some information from him.

According to them, one of his primary emotions right now is guilt, guilt about leaving you without a word."

"I think your psych guys are on the right track," said Bennie. "Yes, he's feeling guilty, and one of the ways a person deals with guilt is to lash out at the person who's causing the feelings. That would be Janice."

"Lash out!" I said, a bit loud, "I'd like to lash out literally against that murderous prick."

"He'll be subtle, Janice," said Bennie. "One of the most devious subtleties is to tell someone, 'I know something that you don't know.' His actions or words will communicate if he knows about the other attacks. Then it's a question of finding out just what he knows."

"You just nailed it on the head, Dr. Ben," said Carlini. "And you, my favorite bullshit detector, will be on the other side of the one-way mirror taking notes."

I wasn't kidding when I made that crack about throwing up on the table. I was really feeling nauseous.

"I have to visit the ladies room," I said, "*NOW.*"

I managed not to throw up. I calmed down, took a few deep breaths, and splashed cold water on my face. Carlini's right. Bennie's right. I've got to do this. I don't consider myself the most courageous person in the world, but I'm not afraid of danger, I'm not afraid to use a gun, or to put myself in harm's way. Seeing and talking to that disgusting husband of mine, on the other hand, scares the hell out of me. What scares me is that I can't imagine what my reaction to him will be. I hope they take my gun away before I enter the visitor's room to meet him.

I returned to the conference table.

"I think you people understand why I'm having such an emotional reaction to this proposal," I said, "but I know how to control my feelings. I'm in, but I'm going to need a lot of support from all of you, especially Bennie."

"You'll get support from all of us, Janice," said Carlini, "but you'll get a lot more than just support from Dr. Bennie. As one of the world's leading experts on psychopathic personalities, he's going to coach you, not just support you. A man who planned the murder of thousands of people qualifies Joseph Monahan as a psychopath, would you not agree, Ben?"

"He absolutely qualifies Mr. Director," said Bennie, "and psychopaths make excellent liars. That's where I come in."

"Okay, folks, it's 1 PM, time to break for lunch," said Carlini. "We'll get together for about one hour after that to lay out an action plan."

"Mr. Director," said Admiral Frank, "a word with you please."

As we all filed out of the conference room, Frank and Director Carlini stayed behind for a few minutes.

"I'm concerned, Bill, really concerned," said Frank. "This morning you introduced me as the deepest mole in the history of American spying. That may be so, but it leaves us with a huge problem. I knew absolutely nothing about al Qaeda's Plan B, and neither did you. If I didn't know about it, how is it possible that anyone else does, and that includes the five guys in prison, most notably Janice Monahan's husband. Janice is a bright, gutsy woman, but that doesn't amount to a pile of dirt if Monahan really knows nothing about the plan. I'm thinking I may need to go back under cover and get inside where I belong."

"Overruled, my friend," said Carlini. "I'll bet serious odds that you already have a target on your back. I can't lose you, and neither can the American people."

"But we've got to get somebody inside – fast. I recommend that you think about who's best for the job. I'll be thinking about it too. We can't put too many bets on a horse named Joseph Monahan."

CHAPTER ELEVEN

Have you ever felt fear, a real deep gut-wrenching fear, but you're not sure what you're afraid of? Director Carlini wants me to meet with my charming husband and pump him for information. I know Bennie will do a great job prepping me for the meeting, but that knowledge is doing nothing for my anxiety.

I'm not in fear of harm, the bodily injury kind. I'll meet Monahan at Leavenworth prison in a controlled environment surrounded by armed guards. He'll be in leg irons no doubt. No, it's worse than that, this fear that's gripping me. Finding out that your husband is traitor and a potential mass murderer is worse than finding out that he's dead. He's the man I once loved and lived with for over 10 years. Then one day he was gone. What I've learned about him since then has removed any trace of affection, respect, or any other positive emotion. Here's a guy who was ready to slaughter thousands of innocent people all in the name of a strange philosophy that he believed was a religion. He really believed, if what I've heard is true, that God was commanding him to kill people. It's not like waking up one day and realizing your husband was a philandering drunk. No, people like that surrender to their weaknesses. Joe Monahan, on the other hand, was ready to commit an unimaginable crime, and willing to do it out of some strange devotion to duty. I don't think I'm being dramatic when I think of him as a living monster.

I think my fear is something that doesn't involve Joe Monahan. I think it involves me, and what I may encounter. The thought of looking at him and speaking to him nauseates me and makes me want to bolt for a bathroom right now.

I think of myself as a pretty rational person. I'm an engineer, a good one, and not the kind of nut who "loses it." But these crazy thoughts keep running through my mind. I won't be armed, of course, but I can be a tough customer if I need to be. I have these fantasies about reaching out and pummeling the bastard, demanding to know how he feels about all of the widows, widowers, and orphans he was about to make.

Bennie, a guy who knows a thing or two about interrogation, has already told me that the setting will likely be me sitting across the table from Monahan. He'll be in shackles I'm sure, but what about me? The cops and everybody else will protect me from him, but who's going to protect him from me.

Okay, I'm venting and I know it. I've discovered in the last few weeks that I really care about other people, that I have a patriotism that I wasn't aware of, and that I have responsibilities way beyond making HVAC systems work. Carlini's right. We have little to go on except for my relationship with a vicious prick named Joseph Monahan. I wish somebody else could do this job, but I'm convinced that I'm the logical choice.

I can handle this. I promised.

CHAPTER TWELVE

B ennie Weinberg here.

I'm stretching my legs and taking a walk around CIA headquarters waiting for our next meeting with Director Carlini. He's a sharp and dedicated guy, and I think he hit this one right on the head, his idea of Janice meeting with her husband.

I have to admit that I'm feeling uncomfortable about this whole thing, especially since I'm right in the middle of it. My job is to coach Janice, along with a lot of input from CIA brass. This isn't going to be easy, given that Janice is revolted by the thought of Joseph Monahan. Another reason it won't be easy is Monahan himself. As you probably know, I'm a maven on vetting witnesses, including psychopaths, for whom lying is as natural as a dog peeing on a fire hydrant. I have no doubt at all that this guy is a psychopath. If he was willing to kill thousands of sailors for some twisted religious belief, I don't doubt that he's ready to lie like a rug to throw us off track. We're all assuming, of course, that he has some actual knowledge of what is supposed to happen.

I like Janice, not that I've known her for a long time. She has guts and brains, and God knows she's beautiful. I wonder if she'd be interested in a short balding guy...but I digress. Janice, because of what she told us about Joseph Monahan, gave us some great leads that helped us stop the Thanksgiving Attacks on the ships. No doubt about it, Janice is one solid human being, and she's about to face a meeting that will be emotionally devastating

My job is to make the meeting less devastating, but also to coach Janice on getting information from a psychopathic scumbag who she used to sleep with. My job is easier than hers.

I hope she's had some acting lessons because she's going to put on the stage debut of her life. Your humble *bullshit detector* is coming up against a man who lives on lies. But I'll be doing my work on the other side of a one-way mirror.

Janice will meet this bastard face to face.

CHAPTER THIRTEEN

Our meeting in Carlini's office resumed at 1:30 PM. I'm not feeling too comfortable about meeting with my psychopathic husband, but I may as well get over it. I'll never feel comfortable with the idea, but I'm sure I'll find out more about the plans now.

Director Carlini brought the meeting to order.

"Okay, folks," said Carlini, "we have to move and move fast. Ben and Janice, do you two think that Janice can be ready for her meeting with Monahan in three days?"

Bennie nodded to me, politely indicating that I should speak first..

"Before we took our break," I said, "I think I made it clear to all of you how I feel about this plan. But at the same time, I have to agree with you. With so little to go on, it's probably best to use my background with Monahan as a way to find information. For the life of me, I don't know how I'll do this, but I guess that's what our friend Dr. Bennie is all about. So, Ben, what's the plan?"

Bennie looked at Director Carlini.

"Can you arrange for an air force jet to take Janice and me to Leavenworth, Kansas tomorrow morning?" Bennie said. "I want to coach Janice in the actual room where she'll meet Monahan, to remove as much surprise and discomfort as possible."

"Consider it done, Ben," said Carlini as he gestured toward his deputy with a face that said, 'make this happen.'

CHAPTER FOURTEEN

The United States Disciplinary Barracks at Leavenworth, Kansas or U.S.D.B at Fort Leavenworth is commonly known as just "Leavenworth." It's actually one of three prisons on the Fort Leavenworth property, but the only one designated "maximum security."

It isn't particularly ugly as far as prisons go, but it gives me the creeps. They tore down the old prison that had been operating since 1874, and put up a modern "state of the art" structure in 2002. On our way here I Googled it on my iPad. Gotta love the home page: "Welcome to the U.S. Disciplinary Barracks." *Welcome?* Why not "Welcome to Hell, You Fiend?"

Besides my charming husband and some 440 other nasties, U.S.D.B. Leavenworth holds murderous luminaries such as Nidal Hasan, the patriotic American army officer who killed 12 and wounded 30 at Fort Hood in 2009. Joe Monahan belongs here.

On the off-hand chance that Monahan may see me, I wore a full burqa, covering my entire body, enabling me to see the world through narrow eye slits.

"You look lovely Janice, I must say," said Ben.

"Stuff it Bennie, I'm nervous enough."

We were greeted by Warden Max Williams, who received a personal call from CIA Director Carlini to announce our visit. Even though we were accompanied by the top guy, we had to go through a symphony of sliding, clashing, banging, beeping, honking, and various other noisy security crap before we arrived at the room where I would meet Joe Monahan in two days.

I didn't know much about interrogation rooms other than from cop shows on TV. Bennie expertly showed me the room's "features," including steel table legs that were bolted to the floor, enabling the efficient shackling of prisoners. A small anteroom would house an armed guard, giving a prisoner/interrogee the false impression that there was privacy. Of course, the guard could hear every word. Along a wall was the famous one-way mirror, enabling a person or group of people to eavesdrop on the conversation. During the actual meeting with my darling husband, Bennie would observe from the other side of the mirror.

Bennie, in his tough NYPD way, then started to show his brilliance as he prepared me for my meeting with Joe Monahan. Doctor Bennie knows so much about the human mind and its devious ways it's almost creepy. I'm glad he's on my side.

"Look, Kiddo," (can't you picture Bennie on *Law and Order*?) "Commander Dickhead is going to work over your mind. Whatever positive thoughts about this guy you ever had, keep them bundled up on the side. He's a deceitful psychopath who knows how to manipulate people, and that includes you. He deceived countless others for 20 years while he plotted to kill them. He had you, his wife, convinced that he was just a career naval officer, a regular guy working his way up the ranks. When Jack Thurber and I first met you at your house, you were clueless that your missing husband may have been a terrorist. Most victims of psychopaths are like that, clueless. They're clueless because the psycho is a master of deception. How many times have you read an account of a serial killer after he'd been nabbed? Reporters would always canvass the neighborhood to ask people what they thought of the suspect. Inevitably you read stuff like, "I can't believe it's him," "But he was such a nice, friendly man," or, "They must have the wrong guy; it couldn't be him."

"Remember John Wayne Gacy?" Bennie continued. "A charming civic-minded guy who invented a character for himself named 'Pogo the Clown.' He'd volunteer for charitable fundraisers, children's parties, and parades. What a guy. Problem was that he sexually assaulted and killed at least 33 kids and buried them in the crawl space under his house. 'But he was such a nice, friendly man.'"

"I'm not saying Joe Monahan is a John Wayne Gacy, at least not in his manner or style. But if the Thanksgiving Attacks happened, his body count would have made Gacy look like an ideal neighbor."

"Bennie," I said, "we may be time travelers but we're not soothsayers. I understand that. But please give me some things to look for, some conversational stuff to identify. Like you've been saying, I really don't know this man. I thought I did, but everything that's happened tells me I was leading a fantasy life with that slime. What do I look for, Bennie?"

"Janice, like you said, we're not soothsayers and we can't predict human actions with scientific accuracy. But, and my darling mother and biggest fan would agree, you're looking at the smartest guy in the world when it comes to this shit. Nobody knows more about people like Joe Monahan than me."

"Bennie," I said, "you don't have to convince me that you're smart, and I'm not saying that to jerk your chain. I've seen you in action. You can observe the human mind in a way that's almost spooky. If you weren't here, I would refuse to be here. But let's get specific, okay?"

"Okay, Janice, let's look at what you can expect from Joe Monahan."

—◄+►—

Bennie then laid out the psychopathic profile of the man I married. Ben is a genius; there's no other way to describe it. He jokingly refers to himself as "Bennie the Bullshit Detector," but that's only because he has a self-deprecating sense of humor. Let's face a disturbing fact: most of what goes on in our heads, including mine, *is* bullshit. It's the way we communicate, with ourselves and others. It's the grand game that we all play. It's the way the world goes round. But this tough cop, Dr. Benjamin Weinberg, MD, Harvard Medical School, has found a way to detect the difference between honest thoughts and actions, and bullshit.

In the ten years I was married to Joe Monahan, the two of us lived a life of bullshit. Now, my good friend Bennie is going to show me how to detect it.

CHAPTER FIFTEEN

"I'm not going to dictate my thoughts to you, Kiddo," said Bennie, "we're going to interact. I'm going to pick your brain and let you come to conclusions and insights. This process works especially well with bright people, and you're one of the brightest people I know."

Bennie can be gruff, but he can also be quite pleasant, especially with a compliment like that. And when something like that comes from Bennie Weinberg, it isn't, well, it's honest.

"Janice, what is the overriding thought in Monahan's mind since we thwarted the attacks and he was arrested?"

"Shame, with a side of guilt." I said.

"Now I'm sure you've had feelings of guilt and maybe even shame in your life," Bennie said. "How do you handle that?"

I thought for a few minutes. "Well," I said, "I'm embarrassed to admit this, but I always try to rationalize it, to find somebody else or something else to blame it on, anybody but myself. Yes, I may have done such and such, but if it weren't for him, or her, or it, I never would have done the thing."

"Janice, you've just described the human condition, something that's hard-wired into our survival instinct. It can't be me who did that. No, I'm the good guy. If I did such a thing I'd be a bad person, and my self-esteem suffers, and then I'm feeling worthless. No, it wasn't me, it was somebody else, or some set of circumstances. I remember the late great comedian, Flip Wilson.

He coined the phrase, 'the devil made me do it.' Yup, shift the blame. And a person who gets really good at shifting the blame becomes a psychopath."

"So, Bennie, who or what do you think Joe is going to blame this on?"

"The literature, including my own contributions, points to people who are close to the psychopath. But let's back off psychopathy for a moment and get back to our simple human condition. A wife asks, 'Why didn't you empty the dishwasher?' The husband says, 'If you didn't give me so many other things to do I would have.' It wasn't me who failed to empty the dishwasher, it was you who prevented me from doing it."

We took a short break while I laughed hysterically. Bennie has a way of describing the human condition so perfectly he should go into stand-up comedy. So a guy blames his wife for *his* not emptying the dishwasher. It's funny, but also it's starting to make me uncomfortable. I think I see what's coming next.

"So, Janice, Who do *you* think your guilt-ridden husband will blame for what he was about to do?"

"Well, there are two obvious candidates. Number one is Admiral Frank, aka Ayham Abboud, the intelligence mole who lied to him for 20 years. The other is me, if for no other reason that I lived with him and, well, your dishwasher analogy is perfect."

"I'll tell you who's number one, Janice. It's you."

"Why me?" Oh shit, notice how I'm trying to shift the blame somewhere else?

"A few reasons, Janice. Number one, Frank's cover, as far as we know, hasn't been blown. All Monahan knows is that 'Sheik Abboud' has been missing. So if the memory of this big brother figure persists, Monahan's not going to blame him. And he's definitely not going to blame his religion, or the perversion of the religion he bought into. No, if it weren't for his sexy heathen wife he would never have been distracted, he would have pulled off his plan. But forget the logic of it. You're the one who will be in front of him, you're the one who will get the blame, or at least a big part of it."

"Bennie, I think you nailed it. He's gonna blame me. So he's a fucking nut case – Is that an apt description?"

"Let's call it a working diagnosis."

"So it's all my fault, fine, it got it. But here's my problem with this whole inquiry. Ben, you're a good shrink, an amazing shrink. But I'm an engineer, a pretty good one if I don't say. I'm trained not just to diagnose problems, but to find solutions. I need to solve problems. So we diagnose his mind as being disposed to blame everything on yours truly. Great, but where does that get us? I believe the problem we're looking to solve is to get Joe Monahan to lead us to where the bombs are. Without that we'll be wasting our time just to give him an emotional catharsis. Bennie, we've got to find the fucking bombs."

"That's where we're going next, Janice. By the way, and I know this sounds strange coming from a foul mouth like me, but I notice your language is getting saltier and saltier."

"Thanks for pointing that out, Ben. I really have to reign in my tongue. I always cuss a lot when I'm frightened. It's immature and stupid. I promise to watch my vulgarity."

"Well, that's a solid piece of self-knowledge. When you're frightened you use vulgar language. Knowing that about yourself is a great thing for your mental health."

"Bennie, if you don't mind me asking, where do you get your delightful potty-mouth speech patterns? Sometimes listening to you is like sitting in a sports bar on payday. Is it a cop thing?"

"Well, Janice, since we're sharing honest details about our subconscious thoughts, I'll be happy to answer your question. I curse to look and sound tough. That's right. I'm a short, chubby, balding intellectual who deals with cops every day. I deal with cops, overworked prosecutors, and a lot of criminals. I don't want them to know that I graduated from Harvard; I want them to know that I'm tough. It's both practical and also a self-deluding defense mechanism. So that's my potty mouth story."

I wouldn't expect anything less than complete honesty from Bennie, my favorite shrink. I'm glad he helped me realize my foul language is an attempt to make the fear go away. But fear is a part of life. It doesn't mean I have to be an obscene loud mouth just because I'm afraid of something. I really have to work on this. Using four-letter words all the time is dumb, immature, vulgar, and disrespectful of other people.

Fuck it, I'm scared.

CHAPTER SIXTEEN

Bennie and I enjoyed a nice dinner of prison slop in the employee's dining room. We had mashed potatoes, at least I think they were potatoes, next to some brown substance with gravy on top, and a side of broccoli that was prepared last month. Even though the room was for prison employees, there were armed guards at the entrance. The lighting was so bright I wished I had sun glasses. Over the sound system wafted the pleasant dinner accompaniment of *Bad Man LeRoy Brown*. I was in the mood for a vodka martini, but it wasn't on the Leavenworth menu.

Tomorrow Bennie and I will finish our psychological profiling of Lieutenant Commander Joseph Monahan, would be mass-murderer and possible source of critical information. We had rooms at the local Holiday Inn, and we both decided it was a good idea to hit the sack early because we had a lot more work to do the next day. I fell asleep watching re-runs of *Criminal Minds*.

The next morning at 8 AM, Bennie and I enjoyed another meal at Chez Leavenworth. I couldn't tell if the scrambled eggs came from a chicken, or maybe a duck, so I stopped speculating and dove into my burnt toast with a side of bacon that was more like beef jerky.

"I understand that prisons are for punishment," I said, "but why do they have to take it out on the employees?"

"Brace yourself Janice. It's called 'empathy training.' The correctional people are supposedly closer to their charges emotionally if they experience some of the same things the inmates go through. Bon appétit."

After breakfast, Ben and I returned to the interrogation room.

"Janice, yesterday you posed the question, the big question. How do we get Monahan to point us to the bombs?"

"You got that right, Bennie. Unless we get that, this whole trip has been worthless bullshit. Whoops, sorry about my language. Oh, fuck it. Where are we going with this, Ben?"

"So we find, or rather you'll find, that Monahan blames all of his problems on you. What happens next is where you acting skills come in. So let me play Joe Monahan in this process. 'Janice, if it weren't for you, if you had only been more attentive, I wouldn't have strayed in such a strange direction. At home, I felt no emotional connection to you. I only found peace in my new religion. A man can't live as an emotional outcast, and that's how you made me feel."

"Your response, Janice? From the gut, if you will."

"Look you weird creep, if you hadn't spent so much goddam time trying to turn me into some kind of Middle Eastern nun, I would have paid more attention to you. Instead of watching TV with me and holding hands, you were in your office listening to Arabic tapes. You created the emotional wasteland, shithead, not me."

"Congratulations, Kiddo. You got the test 100 percent wrong. There's a reason you never see a bullfighter punch a bull in the nose. The matador knows he can win the fight by feints, not confrontation."

"Well, you asked me for my 'gut response,'" I rationalized, shifting the blame to Bennie.

"Yes I did, and thank you for that. But now let's crawl into your bright mind, which is the organ you'll use tomorrow, not your gut. You see, when Monahan starts to unload all of his blame onto you, he'll begin to feel better. I've run experiments on people in situations like this. The instruments actually show that heart rate and blood pressure subside when a person puts off his mistakes onto someone else. Joe Monahan will actually start to feel relaxed. And that's when you invite him to charge your cape, Madam Matador."

"Have I told you recently how smart you are, Bennie?"

"No, but I love to hear it. Better yet, text my mother."

"But exactly how do I wave the cape?"

"Right now, Janice I want you to do something for me. I want you to cry."

"But I'm not feeling sad. How do I just cry?"

"I'm sure you've heard about *method acting*, the way all modern actors perform their roles these days, at least the good ones. It was invented by a guy named Stanislavski, but was brought to the American screen by Lee Strasberg, the actor and director. He's the guy who played the mobster Hyman Roth in *The Godfather.* It's simple, really. The actor drags up a distant memory of something sad, frightening, or funny, and uses the resulting emotions to give a more realistic portrayal of a character. That's what we need you to do."

"Sounds good, Ben, but how?"

"I just told you how. Just do it. Cry."

When I was eight years old I had an adorable calico kitten named Soxy. She loved to chase things as much as she liked to eat. She especially loved to chase balls. While out in our front yard one day, my little brother threw a ball into the street. Soxy took off after it. She hadn't yet caught up with the ball when the front tire of a UPS truck rolled over her. I was looking at her when it happened. I saw the tire roll over her.

I put my face in my hands and started to sob like a baby. Bennie handed me a box of tissues. I could feel my shoulders bouncing up and down, up and down, as the sobs rolled through me like waves; hot, nasty, powerful waves. I didn't want it to continue, so I let my mind wander to other thoughts, pleasant thoughts. I wiped the tears from my eyes, took another couple of honks into the tissue, and looked at Bennie.

"Perfect, simply perfect," said Bennie. "I almost joined you."

"Let me tell you what I thought about, Ben."

"No, no, absolutely not. Whatever it is, it's your private thought, your own private sad little thought. You pull up that thought up whenever you need to. Bring that thought to your mind after Monahan dumps his blame on you. You, madam actress, are going to feel terrible that you were such a miserable woman that you led him to murder thousands of people. If only you knew, if only you realized you weren't tending to his needs, this whole thing never would have happened. What a rotten nasty bitch you are."

"May I puke now?"

CHAPTER SEVENTEEN

I am Sheik Abbas Haddad, the leader of a small army of brothers who will soon bring America to its knees. I have no doubt that the infidels believe they have scored a big success against us. They saved five American aircraft carriers that we were going to destroy in a few weeks. I do have to give my enemy credit for their intelligence. I also give them credit for picking up on small clues and for mobilizing their amazing technology to stop us. I thought our plan was perfect. I was wrong.

But they are fools if they assume that we had only one plan, that we could be defeated in one operation. All they have done is to force us to make their destruction even worse. Instead of destroying a few naval ships, we shall now strike at the heart of this heathen nation, at its most important cities, at the core of what they call their civilization. They named our thwarted ship explosions the Thanksgiving Attacks. What they don't know is that the Thanksgiving Attacks will happen, and will become a living nightmare for this heathen land. On Thanksgiving Day, just over a month from now, the fist of Allah will strike the Americans. The fist will strike at New York City, Los

Angeles, Chicago, San Francisco, and their seat of government in Washington DC.

I am in Denver, Colorado, the city that houses our second bomb assembly plant. The building is much like the one in Detroit from which we intended to launch our attacks on the ships. The structure is smaller than the one in Detroit, but is adequate for our plans.

Seven of my brothers are here at the plant in Denver, a small group, but small for a reason. Secrecy is essential for our attacks to be successful. None of my brothers here at the plant know where we will attack, and they won't know until it happens. The other soldiers in our little army are the men who will drive the bombs to their targets. Even they don't know where they will go until the day before the attacks.

I, along with my colleagues in Yemen, have kept the secrecy so tight that only my superiors in al Qaeda know the plans.

But there is one problem, a serious problem. Abu Hussein, our brother American naval officer known as Joseph Monahan, is in the hands of the infidels. Brother Abu is only one of four people who knows all of the details of our glorious plan. But he is in the American prison known as Leavenworth. I have no doubt that the Americans will torture him and the other naval officers who were captured. They can torture the others all they want, but Monahan is the only one with the knowledge to keep us from our goal. He is a problem that needs a solution.

CHAPTER EIGHTEEN

Bennie here.

It's 8 AM on the morning of the big meeting between Janice and Joseph Monahan. Janice and I are in the interrogation room to rehearse my coaching tips one more time. Her meeting with Monahan is set for 10 AM. I think I'm more nervous than she is. Janice is one solid human being. She'll soon meet with her terrorist husband, the man she once loved, and yet she looks calm. I'd like to take credit for my wonderful coaching skills, but it's Janice who reached inside herself and came up with a carload of courage.

There was a knock on the door, which pissed me off because I had given instructions to the warden that Janice and I should not be disturbed. Janice gave me a "now what?" look. I walked over to the door and opened it.

Both Janice and I shouted at the same time, "Buster!"

Buster is a spy, a high level CIA agent, and a guy both Janice and I had gotten to know and like in our weird recent few weeks. We have no idea how or why he got his nickname Buster, but having seen him in action it seems like an appropriate moniker. His real name is Gamal Akhbar. About six feet tall with a muscular build, Buster is a Coptic Christian born in Lebanon. His appearance is decidedly Arabic, and he speaks the language fluently. Buster was our official CIA team leader when we called ourselves The Thanksgiving Gang. Among Buster's many talents is his ability to conceal his identity when he needs to. He also has a habit, no, more like a well- honed trait, of showing up unexpectedly. The man is a total professional at what he does, and I was happy to see him here with us.

We exchanged high fives and Janice gave him a hug.

"So what have you been up to recently?" I said.

"You know I can't answer that question, Ben."

They don't call these guys spooks for nothing.

"Director Carlini ordered me to come here. I wanted to get here last night but I got sidetracked," Buster said.

"You got sidetracked for reasons you can't disclose," said Janice with a laugh.

Buster shrugged as if to say, "You know me by now."

I brought Buster up to speed on my coaching sessions with Janice, and what we were expecting from Monahan.

"To put it in a nutshell for you, Buster," I said, "I expect to see a man in what I call 'psychological survival mode.' He's been caught, nailed, his plan totally thwarted. A more normal person would feel remorse, maybe even guilt, but this man is not a normal person. This is a cold blooded-killer, or at least that's what he planned to be. Janice's job is to get him to open up. Expect him to pass blame onto Janice, maybe even feel self-righteous about it."

"Bennie," said Buster, "what's the objective here? A psychological drama from Monahan sounds interesting, but what are we really after? I know what it is, but I want to hear it from you."

"The objective is simple," I said. "We want to find the bombs. I want to see any indication at all from this guy that he knows about Plan B, the bombing of the cities. If he does, then we begin serious interrogation. I see this guy as a bomb-sniffing dog."

CHAPTER NINETEEN

S o it's finally going to happen, my meeting with Joseph Monahan, the would-be mass murderer, the man I once loved who turned himself into a terrorist.

Bennie's done a great job of preparing me for this, or I hope he did. At least he cut down on my fear. Yes, I still have some butterflies, but I'm ready to meet this man, this stranger, this mystery. I know what to expect, thanks to Bennie.

It was 10 AM when I heard the door at the back of the room being unlocked. It seems that everything in a prison is preceded by clanging and jingling noises, keys noisily turning locks and bolts sliding.

Two armed guards, each holding one of Joe's arms, escorted him in. As expected, he wore leg irons and his hands were cuffed. One of the guards hooked his handcuffs to a chain under the table, leaving him just enough arm movement to scratch his nose if need be. He wore a bright orange prison uniform. As Ben had coached me, I sat and looked at Joe with as little expression on my face as possible. I was waiting for the smugness, the arrogance that Bennie predicted. Here it comes, I thought, and I'm ready.

But he looked sad, on the verge of tears. He looked like somebody who knew he did something wrong. He put his head down near the table top and stroked his forehead with his shackled hands. He looked like he was feeling guilty. He's not supposed to look this way, I thought.

"Hello, Janice."

"Hi, Joe."

Tears welled up in his eyes as he looked at me, and they streamed down his face. These weren't the kind of tears that just slip loose when you can't hold them in. These were the kind of tears that take over. The tears were in control. There was no stopping them, no way to make them go away. This man was really crying, and I didn't think it was method acting.

"I'm sorry, Honey," Joe rasped, "Goddamit I'm sorry."

Joe then broke into sobs, deep upsetting sobs, the kind of sobs you see in a child who just got spanked. He either couldn't control his crying or didn't want to try. I shoved a box of tissues across the table to him. I'm not a psychiatrist, that would be my friend Ben on the other side of the mirror, but I know enough about people to realize that I was not looking at an act.

I heard Bennie in my ear piece.

"This isn't what I expected, Janice. Roll with it. Tap into your 'method acting' sadness and be sympathetic."

I thought about my childhood kitten, Soxy, and the tire of the UPS truck slowly rolling over her. It worked. In a couple of seconds I joined my husband in a bawling duel.

Our slobbering finally slowed and we were in tear-wiping mode. I was glad I went light on the eye shadow that morning. But I noticed that my "act" wasn't completely an act. Maybe it's a normal human reaction, but it saddened me to see the man I once loved crying his eyes out.

I was on my own. Bennie kept telling my earpiece that I should go by my gut. I decided to see if there was any of that blame shifting that Ben coached me on.

"Joe," I said softly – the scene seemed to require softness, "is there anything I did to drive you away, is there anything I could have done to make things different?"

Joe banged his forehead on the table and shouted, "No, no, no. This was a Joe Monahan operation. You're a beautiful, wonderful woman. You did everything possible to make a good marriage. I blew it, I fucking blew it. Lieutenant fucking Commander Joseph Monahan blew it."

Now, I was really amazed. If there is one thing that Joe Monahan always prided himself on it was his refusal to cuss, unlike me. I don't recall hearing him even say hell or damn. Now he's carpet bombing "f" words almost as much as me.

"I love you, Honey" Joe said, biting his knuckles to avoid crying again. "I love you more than my miserable fucking life."

When he said that, he looked down at the table. I think he didn't want to see my reaction, didn't want to see me not reciprocating his love. Without saying it, we both realized there can be no going back. He's in prison for life, facing a strong chance of the death penalty at his next trial, which will be for treason. Our life together is over and we both knew it. But I can't say that I didn't feel bad for the guy. I like to think of myself as being emotionally tough, but pistol-packing, karate-chopping Janice was sad.

I felt like shit.

CHAPTER TWENTY

Bennie here.

Buster and I have been exchanging pantomime hands up and shoulder shrugs, the meaning of which is, "What the hell is going on here?"

Like any normal self-deceiving human being, I'm trying to come up with reasons why I wasn't wrong. I'm trying to think why my predictions of Joseph Monahan's behavior were so off target. I'm trying to think of reasons why he's acting so completely different than I predicted.

Oh, to hell with it, I was wrong. Simple as that.

But I take consolation in getting right the stuff that I'm famous for, detecting bullshit, and on that count I think I'm doing well. So here's my professional diagnosis. Joseph Monahan is not lying, he's not bullshitting. He's telling the truth. This is not what I expected. But now what?

"Buster, the bad news is that I missed my prediction completely. We're not looking at a blame- shifting psychopath. We're looking at a guy who just yanked down the zipper on his soul. But the good news is that this meeting is better than we could have expected. Whatever this guy's got bottled up seems to be erupting like a volcano. If he's got something to say, he'll say it. Our interrogation may simply consist of asking questions and recording the answers."

"I think we should let Janice keep going," said Buster. "Why put you and me in the mix when Janice has this guy opening up like a thunder cloud?"

"I agree, Buster."

"Janice," I said through her ear piece, "this is going well, amazingly well. Just follow your instincts and keep him talking. I know this is a bit rough on you, but just hang in there."

CHAPTER TWENTY ONE

Bennie and Buster wanted me to continue flying solo and keep Joe Monahan in talk mode. Time to suck it up and do my job. At the end of this day, I thought, I'll need a good workout, a shower, and a Martini, a nice big straight-up Martini.

I started the morning with an objective, to get Joe talking. Then I realized that all I had to do was interject an occasional question and let Joe ramble on. He seemed to want to talk, to do nothing but open up and tell me everything. He kept looking at me with that pitiful look as if he were a dog that peed on the rug and was awaiting the consequences.

For the past few weeks I've hated Joseph Monahan. After I found out he was one of the conspirators I hated him with an intensity I didn't know I had. But as I spoke to him I found it hard not to feel pity. But that's not what I was there for. I was there to see if Joe Monahan could help us avoid the approaching disaster.

"Joe," I said, stepping into the truck-wide breach he had opened, "what happened to you?"

"Janice, Honey, I've been asking myself that question for years."

It must have been 10 years since he's called me "Honey."

"I lost my mind in a belief system that I confused with religion. It all came so natural, one logical building block piling on top of the next one, until there came a time when blowing up an aircraft carrier with 5,000 people on it seemed like a next step, a simple extension of where my mind was heading all those years."

"Did you ever change your mind," I asked, "did you ever question what you were about to do?"

"Yes, I did. I started to have doubts. It started years ago. I have been trained and indoctrinated for years that non-Muslims were heathen, and that the true path of God called on me to do whatever I could to destroy them."

"Destroy them?" I said. "Do you include *me* in the word *them?*"

He started to cry again. I realized that I had to steer this conversation away from emotional issues.

"Yes, you," he said. "Can you believe that my twisted beliefs turned me against you, the woman I love? I thought of you, like the others, as a barbarian. But as the day of the attacks approached, I started to have real doubts. As I did my work aboard ship, I would look at my fellow crewmembers and think about the plan to kill them. I started to wonder who the real barbarian was. Can a just and loving God inflict such suffering? You often took me with you to Mass. In my radical mind I put up with it, although I thought it was an apostasy. But as my doubts crept in I started to read the Bible you kept next to the bed. Then I I met that guy Father Rick Sampson, a good friend of Captain Patterson. I started to like him and we even had lunch a few times. He has such a simple joyous love of God. When I would ask him why he loved Jesus so much, he would say things like, 'Hey, Jesus loves me, and he loves you, so I'm just reciprocating.' When I asked him if Jesus helped him, he said that he couldn't live without Jesus. I remember Father Rick's favorite expression, 'Give it up for God.' Father Rick lives a religion of joy."

"Janice?"

"Yes, Joe."

"Would it be possible for me to see Father Rick again?"

"I will try to make that happen," I said. I meant it.

"But Joe, were you prepared to carry through with the plan even though you started having doubts?"

"No, absolutely not. I wasn't going to go through my part of it, and I had begun to take steps to make sure none of the other Navy men did their jobs. You Thanksgiving Gang people thwarted the plan, but I would have stopped it if you hadn't."

I hoped Bennie was in high alert on the other side of the mirror. There was no diagram for how this conversation was supposed to go, so I figured that it was time to get to the most important issue of all, the upcoming attacks.

"Joe, do you know anything about another series of Thanksgiving Attacks, a Plan B, so to speak?"

"Janice, you've come to the most important question of all. The answer is yes, I do know about the upcoming attacks. If I may make a suggestion?"

"Go ahead, Joe."

"I assume that on the other side of that one-way mirror are agents of the FBI or the CIA. May I suggest that they join us? There isn't much time before the attacks."

CHAPTER TWENTY TWO

Within 30 seconds of Joe's suggestion, Ben and Buster walked in. I was glad to have some professional firepower in the room. Introductions were obviously up to me. Before they came into the room Buster said into my ear piece that I was not to tell Joe that Bennie is known as the Bullshit Detector.

"This is Benjamin Weinberg, a detective with the NYPD and currently Deputy Agent with the CIA. Agent Gamal Akhbar is a senior CIA Agent. We call him Buster."

Because Joe's hand shackles prevented him from extending a hand, or even standing up, they all just nodded toward each other. I moved my chair to the right to enable Buster and Ben to sit directly across from Joe.

⇥⇤

"Mr. Monahan," said Buster, "we're hoping that you can help us prevent an unthinkable disaster. From what we've heard, I think you may be the key to stopping the attacks. My first question involves your position with al Qaeda. Are you a leader or do you hold the same status as the other naval officers?"

"Yes," said Joe. "I am in a leadership position, I'm ashamed to admit. I know much more detail than the other officers."

"Do you know where, when, and how the plan will be executed?" said Buster. "Do you know where the bombs are?"

"No, I don't know where the bombs are."

Bennie tapped Buster on the sleeve, signaling that he wanted to ask the next question. Bennie had caught a whiff of bullshit.

"Mr. Monahan," said Bennie, "you say that you're in a leadership position, but yet you say that you don't know the most important part of the puzzle, where the bombs are. Please explain."

"Gentlemen, al Qaeda has been studying the American military and law enforcement for years. In the Navy, as well as the CIA, there's a critical doctrine known as 'need to know.' You guys are totally familiar with this rule, I'm sure. It's a simple but important part of security. The fewer people who know a secret, the less the chance of it being leaked. Plan B has not yet been fully explained to me. I can tell you that the plant that holds the bombs is similar to the one in Detroit, only somewhat smaller. I can also tell you that the bombs have a much higher yield than the one- kiloton weapons meant for the ships. The Plan B bombs are 10-kilotons, close to the size of the Hiroshima bomb. They are also suitcase nukes, each one weighing about 100 pounds. But the one thing that I do not know, because I didn't yet have the *need to know,* is where the bombs are located."

"Mr. Monahan," Buster said, "sometimes problems are solved or at least uncovered by the smallest bits of information. Please think, is there anything that came to your attention in the past few months that may be significant, even if you don't understand it. Countless innocent people will die unless we can find the answer."

"Believe me sir, I want to help. I don't want blood on my hands; I don't want the dead weighing on me. But I can only give you the information I have."

Bennie was staring at Joe so intently I thought he'd burn a hole in his head. He was scribbling notes so fast I thought his pad would catch on fire.

I decided to weigh in.

"We used to play chess a lot," I said. "I've never been able to beat Joe. He memorized the board. Also, if I ever mentioned to him that I was missing something and I thought it may be in the basement, Joe would be able to locate it in an instant in his mind. When it comes to objects, words, or images, Joe has a photographic memory."

Buster then looked at Joe and each of us.

Joe rubbed his face, his shackles tinkling as he did so. Buster started to ask him a question, but Joe closed his eyes and held his hands palm out as if to say, "please let me think."

"Wait, wait, wait," said Joe in a loud voice. "I have no idea of the location, but I definitely recall seeing an aerial photograph of the 'Plan B' bomb plant. Do you have any graph paper? I can sketch it for you."

I'm never without graph paper. Call me nuts, but to pass time I often sketch industrial designs of a project I'm working on. I handed Joe a piece of graph paper. Bennie opened the table drawer and found a pencil.

"Okay," said Joe, "I've got a clear image in my mind of what the area looked like."

I noticed Buster suddenly lean back, crack his knuckles, and stare at the ceiling, smiling. He looked like a guy who just won a poker hand.

"Janice," Monahan said, "You're the engineer. I'll describe the images and you do the drawing."

One of the structures, apparently a tank of some sort, was round, it's diameter almost as wide as the width of the bomb plant. We were all thinking the obvious: satellite images. The more details in the drawing, the easier to detect it from space or from a surveillance drone.

I chimed in, giving my perspective as an engineer.

"Joe, can you give us any idea about the dimensions of what I'm drawing?"

"Yes," said Joe, "I do know that the width of the plant is exactly the same width as the Detroit building. The visual ratios of all the other buildings and structures are correct; they're burned into my memory."

"Bingo," I yelled. "We've found the Rosetta Stone! We have an image of what the place looks like from above."

Buster splashed some cold water on my enthusiasm.

"We're a hell of a lot closer than we were a few minutes ago," said Buster, "But I remind you that this is a gigantic country. Satellites are great, but the amount of data we have to sift through is enormous."

Buster then announced it was time for a break. He wanted to scan the drawing and send it to his team at CIA headquarters.

CHAPTER TWENTY THREE

I called Max Williams, the warden, and asked if we could have a few sandwiches delivered. The CIA Director had clued him in that we were involved in something critical, and that he may have to bend a few rules. Max is a team player and couldn't be more helpful, even though room service isn't on the normal list of Leavenworth amenities.

Buster called to the guard and told him to unshackle Joe's hands. The guard cleared it with the warden and unleashed our talkative prisoner.

Joe seemed pleased to be uncuffed, as he massaged his wrists and thanked Buster. Then Buster reminded him that we're all armed, so it really wasn't much of a security breach. Joe actually laughed.

⊶⊷

Before we broke for lunch, Ben, Buster, and I huddled for a quick conference out of Joe's hearing range.

"Bennie," said Buster, "next to Monahan, you're the most important guy in this building. Tell us, Dr. Bullshit Detector, are we hearing the truth?"

"Like I always tell people," Bennie said, "my job is to find out if the witness believes what he's saying. If he doesn't, he's lying. I have a 12-part checklist of things I look for, including eye contact, perspiration, hand movements, vocal inflections and other key ingredients. I could go under oath right now and put my medical license in escrow. This guy is telling the truth. No bullshit whatsoever. If he's lying, your friendly shrink, Bennie Weinberg, has met his match.

After lunch, we planned to learn a lot more about what my husband knows. I think we'd all like to hear his thoughts on Frank Thompson, aka Ayham Abboud. I knew I did. Bennie thinks Monahan seemed comfortable with me, and wanted me to continue to be a part of the interview.

Buster agreed. Well I'm glad Bennie thinks Joe feels comfortable with me. I'm still adjusting to this whole surreal experience about me being in the same room as Joe, a man who, until today, I deeply hated. I'm about to play the heavy again, and the knot in my stomach tells me so. Once again, I'm frightened, I admit it. I better watch my tongue. Fear turns my language obscene. No shit.

Buster decided to leave Joe unshackled for the rest of the meeting. Good move I thought. He seems to open up more with his hands free, which should come as no surprise.

CHAPTER TWENTY FOUR

"Joe," I began, "please tell us what you know about a man named Ayham Abboud."

"I've known him for over 20 years, ever since I was a high school senior. As you all know from your investigations, four other American kids and I went on a school trip to Riyadh, Saudi Arabia in 1994. The trip was run by an outfit called *The Center for Open-Minded Youth* and funded, I later learned, by the government of Saudi Arabia."

"Do you have any thoughts you'd like to share about *The Center for Open-Minded Youth*?" I asked.

"Sure," said Joe. "It was really nothing more than a brainwashing organization, a little group designed to foster homegrown American moles, future terrorists. Dr. Weinberg, as a psychiatrist you would be impressed by the many ways they infiltrated our minds."

"Was Ayham Abboud one of the mind infiltrators?" I asked.

"Ayham Abboud has always been a mystery to me, although I really liked the guy and looked up to him like he was my big brother.

The other kids did as well. Ayham was just a few years older than us, spoke perfect English; well, he was American, and was able to relate to all of us, and us to him. I'd have to say that he was one of the mind infiltrators, but there was something about the man that just seemed so natural. I know this sounds crazy, given all the evidence, but I always felt that he was just going through the motions, like he had an agenda that was different from what it appeared to be."

"Did you see him over the years, or was Riyadh your last contact with him?"

"Oh, definitely I saw him, at least twice a year. He was the one who convinced all of us that we should become naval officers, our alternate identity. In the early years we didn't know why, but about two years ago we learned of the Thanksgiving plot. When he told me about the operation, he seemed almost deadpanned, like he was delivering words somebody else gave him. So he introduced me to a future of mass murder, and it was then that I began to have doubts. I should hate the guy, and this is going to sound completely insane, but I still kind of like him.

To tell you the truth, I have a sneaking suspicion that he didn't want the attacks to happen either. Just a gut feeling, but it's there."

"Beside your gut feeling, Joe, is there any objective reason that you think Abboud may have turned against the plan?"

"Well, yes, definitely yes, an objective reason."

"What's that?" I asked.

"He's missing, disappeared, gone. He was supposed to be one of the top men in the plot, but about a month ago he just vanished."

"Was the al Qaeda leadership concerned about his disappearance?"

"Concerned? They went nuts. Look, there are two possible explanations. One, he could have been killed by the CIA."

Joe looked at Buster, who didn't blink or say a word.

"The second possibility is that he was taken out by al Qaeda, and they're just faking their worries about him. From what I could tell, he knew everything about the operation. If he's alive, I hope he realizes that there's a big target on his back."

"Do you know that for certain," Buster interjected, "or are you speculating?"

"Just speculating. Again, 'need to know' is the policy. So, anyway, I hope he's okay. I know it sounds weird, but there's something about the guy that I still like to this day."

"He's doing just fine," said Buster.

What did I just hear? Bennie and I looked at each other like we just saw, or heard, a ghost. Frank's identity is supposed to be Tippety Top Secret, and here's Buster telling Joe that he knows "Abboud" is alive. Well, Buster's the boss and this is his call.

Joe looked at Buster wide-eyed, more surprised by what he just heard than Bennie and me.

"I'm sure it's out of my place to ask," said Joe, "but if I may, how do you know that Ayham is alive and well. Do you have him in custody?"

"Yes, it is out of your place to ask," said Buster. "You will learn more soon."

We'd been talking for six hours, and it was 4 PM. Buster announced that it was a wrap for today.

"Okay, folks, we have a lot of work to do. We're going to meet with Mr. Monahan again soon, but for now we're going to call it a day."

"Joe, I'll be in touch with you shortly," said Buster. "Before 10 AM this morning I thought of you as a terrorist killer. Whatever brought about your awakening, I just thank God it happened."

"If you don't mind," I said, "I just have one more question, based on what Buster just said. Was there one thing that convinced you to turn away from terror?"

"Yes, there was one primary motivation for my awakening, one person. His name is Sheik Abbas Haddad and he is now in charge of the operation. I've observed his actions and speeches over the years.

He's a man who kills for the love of killing, as ruthless a human being as you can imagine. Unlike me, he is a man without doubts."

"I've heard of him," said Buster.

Our meeting with Joe Monahan finally came to a close. He was led away by the guards after we exchanged what can only be described as a friendly goodbye. Buster reminded him that we would need to talk to him again soon.

"Okay folks," said Buster, "our plane, via Air CIA is waiting for us at the airport. We'll fly directly to Langley. Get some sleep on the flight, because we'll be meeting with Director Carlini as soon as we get there."

Buster made a quick secure briefing call to Director Carlini, who likes to know in advance what a meeting is all about. After this mess is over, you will have to pay me a lot of money to sit in another meeting.

CHAPTER TWENTY FIVE

The meeting I dreaded finally happened. Seeing my husband was an event that had me scared out of my wits. Thank God for Bennie for helping to make it a bit more tolerable. But when we all got the shock, the shock that Joe Monahan had actually turned and wanted to help us, we were in a state of stunned disbelief. My fear of meeting him has now been replaced with a strange numbness. I'm emotional roadkill.

I've always loved animals and feel terrible whenever I see one suffer, whether it's a dog, a bird, or a squirrel. I guess that goes for human animals as well. I saw Joe suffering, and although I deeply hated him before the meeting, I now feel a strange sadness.

I also feel a sense of completion. Besides hating Joe Monahan, I was also tearing myself apart. After all, I was the one who married the guy. But after our meeting I know that I married a man who went astray, big time, but he's also a man who has a heart and decided to reclaim his humanity and help prevent suffering, not cause it.

I no longer hate Joe Monahan. I no longer love him, nor do I even like him, but I respect him as a human being. I respect him for having turned his weird life around.

I think that's completion.

CHAPTER TWENTY SIX

I am Sheik Haddad, and I relish the thought that our day of glorious jihad will soon be upon us. The infidels cannot stop this plan, no matter how hard they try. There will soon be explosions of love and justice.

But I worry about Ayham Abboud, the brother that no one has seen in weeks. I also am concerned about Abu Hussein, the naval officer in prison. Brother Hussein knows almost as much about our plan as I do. He knows everything except the location of the bomb plant. But he does know the plans, he does know the details, and he's in the hands of the devious infidels who are torturing him at this moment for information.

Brother Hussein, the man they call Joseph Monahan, must die.

CHAPTER TWENTY SEVEN

Late October was beginning to act like November. As we walked the short distance to the entrance of CIA Headquarters, a stiff wind blew a confusion of leaves across our path. It was cold, not "nippy," but cold. The air temperature was 45 degrees, but with the wind it felt like it was in the 30s. At 7:45 PM it was pitch black. I consoled myself with the thought that daylight savings time and the beginning of spring was only five months away. But then I realized that it's October 21 and Thanksgiving Day is only five weeks away. A shudder went down my back, and accompanied me into the CIA building. The shudder was not because of the cold wind.

A guard opened the door as Ben, Buster, and I headed for our meeting with Carlini. Director Carlini's deputy, Ollie Blake, met us at the door to hustle us through the ringing, clanging, beeping bullshit of security.

"You folks look tired," said Carlini, as we filed into his office. He was nice enough to have arranged a full coffee service along with water, soft drinks, and light snacks.

Tired? I don't recall ever being this exhausted. Meeting for hours with one's estranged husband can be stressful enough, but when said husband is a newly reformed mass murderer serving a long prison term, it makes tiredness and sore muscles a palpable ache. Carlini then said something I thought I'd kiss him for.

"I just want an executive summary of the most important points, and make this meeting fast." said Carlini. "We'll meet longer tomorrow. Buster, please go ahead. If anybody wants to jump in, please do so."

"If you don't mind, Mr. Director, I'm going to offer a conclusion: we've got to get Monahan out of Leavenworth as soon as possible. I would prefer right now, but tomorrow morning would be great. I recommend that we put him up here in a secure apartment and guard him 24 by 7."

"Do you think he's in danger?" Carlini asked.

"Yes, sir. The three of us have spent an amazing day. It seems that Joseph Monahan, Abu Hussein, has changed. He's a born-again anti-terrorist, who's rediscovered his long forgotten American patriotism. No canary could outtalk this guy."

"Here's the summary," Buster continued. "We don't yet know the location of the bombs, but we have a detailed engineering sketch which I've already emailed to my team upstairs to begin satellite recon. We know the guy who's in charge, that homicidal maniac, Abbas Haddad. And we also know an important thing: Monahan is a pretty high-up guy, just shy of being called a Sheik. We know it, but the critical thing is that *they* know it as well. They know Monahan is in prison, and I'll bet they think we're torturing him for information. Carve this in stone, Mr. Director, they're gonna whack Joseph Monahan."

"I see your concern, Buster, but Leavenworth is the most secure prison in the country. How could they possibly get at him there?"

"Mr. Director, some, maybe hundreds, of Monahan's fellow prisoners at Leavenworth are of the jihadi persuasion. Given enough concentrated intention, it doesn't take too much to kill a man in prison. We need this guy, and we have to talk to him more and then some more after that. If we leave him there and visit him a lot, that will set off alarms all over al Qaeda and their operatives at Leavenworth. So I suggest that we create a story, that Monahan got killed in prison. I know just the journalist who will break it. We'll make it realistic and believable and give it to all the newswires. Even al Qaeda won't try to kill a dead man. We gotta get him out of there. We need him here, now."

"Okay, done, sold. I'll make it happen."

Carlini picked up the phone and hit a speed dial number.

"Get me Director Watson, please, William Carlini of the CIA here."

Wow, this is a man of action. Almost restores my faith in the federal government. Almost.

"Sarah, Bill Carlini here. I won't bore you with the details but here's what needs to happen. There's a prisoner at Leavenworth, Joseph Monahan, one of the naval terrorists. We need to get him out of Leavenworth now and bring him here to Langley. Bottom line is that he's turned and is now our best source of information about the upcoming Thanksgiving event. We're concerned for his safety. We know that he'll come more than willingly. He's refused to lawyer up and is totally cooperative. Will you please smooth this over with the Attorney General? Great, I'll call the White House myself."

I'm not believing this. Ever since 9/11 there's been a lot more cooperation between the FBI and the CIA, but this is like a couple of poker buddies calling out for sandwiches.

"Fred Mulroony, please. Bill Carlini here. Hey Fred, I got something that needs to happen, fast."

Now he's on the phone with the White House Chief of Staff. In two minutes he had the official White House Seal of Approval. Mulroony told him that he would personally clear it through the Bureau of Prisons.

At certain levels of government you find people who really believe in getting things done, people who are ass-kickers by nature and aren't afraid of getting yelled at. They're a rare breed, but the country couldn't function without them. I just watched that happen in front of my eyes. If this was handled by low level functionaries, it would be six months before Joseph Monahan was released from Leavenworth, six months too late. Now, he'll fly to CIA Headquarters in the morning. The last thing I needed today was another meeting, but this was exciting.

CHAPTER TWENTY EIGHT

Joe Monahan here.

Today is October 22, six days since I was arrested. I'm on a flight from Leavenworth Prison to CIA Headquarters in Langley, Virginia. Yesterday was the most amazing day of my life. I talked to my beautiful wife, Janice. Well actually I was interrogated by her along with a CIA agent and a police psychiatrist. Although we still lived together until recently, Janice and I had become estranged. That's the wrong way to put it. I caused us to be estranged and I drove her away from me emotionally because of my insane devotion to a cause, a cause of death and destruction, a cause that made me lose my mind and soul.

It's hard for me to believe that over the past 20 years I had become a radical fundamentalist in the service of a twisted ideology, an ideology that advertises itself as a religion. On Thanksgiving Day, just six weeks from the day I was arrested, I was to be a key player in an operation to kill 26,000 innocent people, about 5,200 on my ship alone. That's right, slaughter 5,200 people with a nuclear device, 5,200 people, many of whom I knew personally. I was the ship's weapons officer, an important position on the ship. My fellow crewmembers had no idea that I was soon to betray my country, betray them, and kill them. My wonderful wife didn't know this either. At least it wasn't in the plans to kill her.

For 20 years I was nurtured as a jihadi, a warrior in the cause of radical Islam. I remember seeing an autobiography written by the famous comedian Sid Caesar entitled *Where Have I Been* ? It was about his years as an alcoholic, years that Caesar felt had robbed him of a big part of his life. I can sympathize with that, because that's exactly what I'm thinking, "Where have I been?"

Alcohol has never been a problem with me, but something else robbed me of my mind and soul just as efficiently as alcohol has robbed others. My mind accepted a belief system that called for killing and depriving people of fundamental rights. Notice how I say, "my mind accepted," as if it were some bodily organ separate from my identity. I guess I'm rationalizing, trying to tell myself that it was some other force that caused me to become a potential killer, something that would allow me to duck responsibility.

I've been having doubts about my beliefs for years. The doubts began with 9/11, seven years after my "conversion" to Islam in 1994 at a youth indoctrination camp in Saudi Arabia. Jihadis the world over rejoiced the thrashing of America by sending suicide fighters to crash planes into buildings. Almost 3,000 innocent deaths – for what?

My doubts mounted over the years, but I never shared them with my fundamentalist "colleagues." My mind kept fighting me, my mind kept asking questions, but I moved along, robot-like, toward my mission of death. In the last year my doubts began to harden into mental resistance. And now, although nobody will believe this and I don't expect them to, I had renounced the mission. The Thanksgiving Attacks on the carriers would never happen if I had anything to do with it.

I've heard all about this time travel business ever since the attacks were thwarted a short time ago. I've heard that my captain's husband, the famous writer and reporter Jack Thurber, had traveled two years into the future and learned about the attacks. He and others who were with him have discussed the idea that the Thanksgiving Attacks actually did happen, only in a different realm of time. If that's true, there is some alternate universe where a homicidal maniac named Joseph Monahan actually went through with his barbaric mission. But that isn't me. I renounced the mission. Had the attacks not been prevented by the operation known as Tango Delta, I, Joe Monahan, would have stopped them myself. But I'll never say that in court, where I'll soon be tried for treason. They'll probably give me the death penalty. I deserve it.

In a few weeks the next Thanksgiving Attacks, Plan B, are scheduled to be executed. I want to do anything in my power to prevent them, but there's a problem. I don't know where the bombs are. Al Qaeda works on a "need to know" basis of security. It was not yet my time to know the location of the bombs, but that time would have come shortly. I was an insider, a cog in the workings of the plots.

My life now has one purpose, to save my country. Yes, America, *my* country, the country founded and governed by the rule of law, by compassion and justice, a country where innocent people aren't slaughtered because of some primitive ideology. How I could turn my back on my country, not to mention my incredible wife, is a mystery that will go with me to my grave.

But now it's my duty to stop the operation. It's a duty of atonement for the 20 years I spent as a killer-in-waiting.

The plane just landed and soon I'll be at CIA headquarters. I'm not nervous, but I'm anxious, anxious to get going, to do what we need to do to make Thanksgiving a day of thanks for real.

Obviously my presence here is hush-hush. Before getting out of the car I was given a wig, a fake beard, a hat, and even pillows stuffed into my shirt to make me look heavier. I feel like that gangster Frank

(*Frankie Five Angels*) Pentangeli in *The Godfather*, disguised as a general so he could testify against the mob in court.

I was taken to a door at the rear of the building, an entrance apparently reserved for clandestine comings and goings. My Marine guards told me to keep my hands in my pockets to conceal the fact that my wrists were shackled to a chain that ran around my waist.

We entered the door and walked down a long corridor that had no adornments of any type on the walls, except for exit signs and fire safety stickers. I guess this is a place where, when they take the blindfolds off, you have no idea where you are.

We entered a conference room about 20 feet by 30 feet. Well, it's really an interrogation room, a fact tipped off by the room length mirror, a one-way mirror no doubt. Just like the corridor, the walls were bare, obviously to keep an interrogee's mind from wandering while being questioned.

My removal from Leavenworth was so sudden, I didn't have breakfast, nor was any offered on the plane. I was delighted to see a tray of assorted wraps and sweets, along with fresh coffee, sodas, and water. It was 11:45 AM and I was starving. My Marine guards brought me to my seat and shackled my legs to the floor. To my surprise they removed my handcuffs. I guess they didn't worry that I'd throw food around the room.

"Enjoy your lunch, sir," said one of my guards as he slid the tray in front of me. He didn't know who I was, but the "sir" told me he thought I was important, or maybe he was just polite by nature.

I scoured the array of food and immediately picked out a ham wrap, about as non-halal as you can get.

I was half way through my sandwich when the door opened.

"Good morning, Joe," said Buster, my CIA interrogator from yesterday.

"Good morning, Buster. Please, join me for lunch."

"Don't mind if I do," said Buster. "It's been such a busy morning the only thing I've eaten was a stick of gum."

"What are you having?" Buster asked, always the spook.

"Ham," I muffled through a mouthful.

Buster smiled, the smile of a man who just got an answer he was hoping for.

⊶ ⊷

"Joe, at the risk of repeating myself from yesterday, it's hard to exaggerate how important your cooperation has been. I'd like to ask you a personal question. Maybe it's a rehash of yesterday, but I want to hear it again. Have you converted?"

"Well, converted is a tough question, Buster, because it begs the question, 'converted to what?' But I can tell you this, I am no longer a fundamentalist jihadi. Frankly, I'm no longer a Muslim, an admission that could get my head chopped off in some circles. I'm a guy who has renounced 20 years of blind faith to a weird ideology. Also, I can tell you that I've rediscovered something I was born with. I'm an American. And please believe me when I tell you this, I'm a patriot. I love this country and I'm willing to die to save it."

"As you know, Joe, we don't have a hell of a lot of time. Today is October 22. Thanksgiving is just over a month away, and we're not out of the woods yet. We still have to locate the bombs. The sketch that Janice made from your recollections is an enormous help, but we still have to locate the weapons. When we do find them, it will be your memory and Janice's sketch that nails it."

I felt good, proud even. For years I used my knowledge to plan the destruction of my country. Now I'm helping to save it.

"Before I go," said Buster, "there's somebody I'd like you to meet."

CHAPTER TWENTY NINE

"Joe, I'd like you to meet Frank Thompson, Rear Admiral, United States Navy."

I looked at the man and shook his extended hand. My face felt numb and my heart pounded like a speedboat crashing over waves. I began to perspire, so I reached for a handful of napkins and blotted the sweat from my face. In my life, I've never experienced an episode of syncope or fainting, but the strangest feeling washed over me, and I felt myself starting to lose consciousness. Buster reached over and waved smelling salts under my nose as if he expected my reaction.

"I'll leave you folks to chat," said Buster as he walked out the door.

"Sheik Abboud," I mumbled, "Sheik Ayham Abboud."

"Hello, Joe, nice to see you. I didn't think you'd recognize me without the beard."

That deep sonorous baritone voice was there. Those intense, gazing eyes. His height, his build, even his handshake. All except the beard, and of course, the turban. It's hard to describe how I felt, sort of like walking into a room and seeing a purple elephant dancing with a unicorn.

"Did he say you're an Admiral, an American Navy Admiral?"

"Yes he did, and yes I am. United States Naval Academy, class of 1991. Mind if I have a sandwich, I'm famished."

Sheik Thompson or Admiral Abboud, whatever, reached for the remaining ham wrap.

"My legs are shackled to the floor, Sir," I said, "would you mind getting me some paper towels with cold water."

"Sure thing, Joe. Here you are. By the way, just call me Frank."

"I've known you for 20 years, Frank (God that feels so weird to say) but I just met you three minutes ago. I feel like my head is going to explode."

"Okay, Joe, I think it's obvious that you would like an explanation. I'm what is known as a mole, a deeply imbedded spy. CIA Director Carlini insists that I'm the deepest mole in American history. The U.S. intelligence apparatus, including the CIA, FBI, Naval Intelligence, and just about every other intelligence agency came to a conclusion in the early 90s, shortly after the first bombing of the World Trade Center, that we needed to get inside al Qaeda, deeply inside. We were up against, and obviously still are, an enemy we never knew before, a secretive enemy that chalks up as political success the killing of innocent human beings. Because my appearance is Middle Eastern, owing to my Lebanese mother, I was tapped to be the deep spy, the mole. I was a naval officer on loan to the CIA."

"Were you a CIA operative when I first met you in 1994?" I asked.

"Yes, Joe, I was."

"But Sheik, Frank, whatever, you were one of the people who indoctrinated us. You really seemed to believe what you were saying. Are you telling me now that it was all an act?"

"Yes, Joe, it was an act. It was just like the naval officer act you've been practicing for the past 20 years. We were quite familiar with *The Center for Open-Minded Youth* for many years. It was, and is, I think you'll agree, a brainwashing operation, the purpose of which is to indoctrinate kids like you and your friends were in 1994. And make no mistake about it, *The Center for Open-Minded Youth* works. I'm going to tell you a small part of something that's deeply classified, something we've been studying for years. Here it goes: of the people who have been labeled domestic terrorists by the government, 80 percent of them came through indoctrination at *The Center for Open-Minded Youth*. Yup, 80 percent of our home-grown radicals got their basic training at that lovely school in Riyadh. You'd recognize a lot of the names, but I can't tell you any of them because it's Top Secret. Many of them have been killed over the years, and a lot more are in prison."

"But you seemed so committed," I said. "You seemed to believe the things you told us."

"As I said, Joe, I was trained to act. The purpose of my mission was to take a small group of kids and groom them for something big. By doing that, we hoped to shine a bright light on al Qaeda's plans for major operations, operations such as the Thanksgiving Attacks. And we succeeded, to a degree. The Thanksgiving Attacks on the ships, as you well know, were stopped. I also know that you planned to try to stop them before you were arrested."

"How could you possibly know that?" I said. "It's true, but how could you have possibly known?"

"Joe, you've met Buster, a good man and a great spy. But I promise you, you've never met a spook like me. I know things about you that you probably don't know yourself. And yes, I intend to let my knowledge of your plans be known in a Top Secret court hearing. I'm certain that your sentence will be commuted, whatever the sentence will be. You've redeemed yourself, Joe Monahan. You're a good American."

"So I was a tool, the only good way to put it."

"Exactly, Joe, an unwitting tool. But if I may, I will take credit for your being alive. If it weren't for me and the CIA's big plan to uncover a major plot, you probably would have been one of the people killed or captured. By now, you'd be either dead or in Guantanamo."

"Frank, my mind is a fucking jumble, pardon my Arabic. I've heard recently that the only reason people knew about the Thanksgiving Attacks came from the research that a reporter named Jack Thurber uncovered. I've heard, and this sounds insane, that he time traveled, yes time traveled into the future and found out that the five ships had been destroyed, that the Thanksgiving Attacks did occur."

"Joe, I've met Jack Thurber and I know his wife, who was your commanding officer, quite well. He's got a great reputation, and for a lot of reasons some people in high places believe that he's time traveled. His wife, Captain Patterson, calls him The Time Magnet. It seems that this Jack Thurber has turned the phenomenon of time travel into a tool of espionage, and it's not just airy fairy fiction."

"How can you say it's not fiction?"

"I've done it myself, Joe. I've been to the future and learned of Plan B, the attacks that are planned on American cities. I've been to a future where those attacks were actually history."

"So did I participate in the attacks on the American ships?"

"Joe, in some alternate universe, maybe. A lot of people have experienced time travel recently, but I don't think any of us really understands it. But all I know is the Joe Monahan sitting in front of me, the Joe Monahan who cooperated so much with Buster, is Joe Monahan, the good guy, the patriot. We're gonna stop this thing, Joe."

CHAPTER THIRTY

Janice here.

After all this lunacy is over, I think I'm going to write a novel, if only to create a reality that seems like it makes sense. I'm going to create a bunch of likeable characters who do things like shop for groceries, get flat tires, catch colds, and watch TV. They're all going to have engaging personalities and nice senses of humor, but they'll all be somewhat boring. The most dramatic plot point you're likely to see is *who found the lost beagle*. Hey, that would make an interesting series, *Nancy Delancy, Beagle Hunter*. Nancy Delancy, you see, runs a beagle rescue shelter in Peoria, Illinois. She meets a handsome young man one day who is almost in tears. It seems his pet beagle, Phred, which he adopted from the shelter a month earlier, isn't housebroken, and the handsome young man is beside himself. Nancy, realizing that the clock is ticking, springs into action to solve the crisis, and maybe get a date with Mr. Handsome. A neat and exciting plot twist is just when Nancy thinks Phred has learned his manners, the handsome young man discovers that Phred has been taking clandestine poops under the furniture all the while. Can you feel the tension?

Yes, those are the kind of stories I want to write, ordinary people with everyday problems, with no need for Maalox.

And the one thing my characters will never, ever do, is fucking time travel. And the books will contain no profanity.

So yesterday gets added to my growing collection of amazing days. I actually met my imprisoned husband Joe, who I have been referring to recently, and somewhat unfairly, as a murdering scumbag. It really seems like he's turned a corner, more like a complete about-face.

Until a few months ago he was a bloodthirsty creepy jihadi. Now he's an emotionally open guy who wants to set things straight and divulge all sorts of important intelligence to help his country. This is good, because our country faces a possible nuclear disaster in less than a month.

So I'm happy that I no longer hate my soon to be ex-husband. I will no longer call him a scumbag. But time has passed, and our time together has passed.

CHAPTER THIRTY ONE

I was in an editorial meeting at The Washington Times, when my beeper went off.

"Hi Buster, it's Jack. What's up?"

"Jack, I need you here at Langley, *NOW.*"

"Buster, I know it's only about 10 miles, but traffic is wicked this morning. It may take me 45 minutes or more."

"Jack, look out the window and tell me what you see."

"Well, the big lawn in front of the building."

"Anything going on, Jack?"

"Well, now that you mention it, there's a helicopter landing on the lawn."

"The chopper's for you, Jack. I'll see you in about ten minutes – Director Carlini's office."

⊶+⊷

I walked through the main entrance to the CIA building and was met by Buster himself. We cleared the security check points easily. Buster

93

has a lot of sway around here. He looked nervous, and I can't blame him. He's the lead agent on this mission, probably the most important mission any CIA agent ever faced. Buster and I walked into his small office. He's an extremely neat guy. His desk is empty of paper, with only a single folder on top. As Buster always likes to tell us, a clean desk is like a clean deck, always ready for action.

"Jack, I need you to write a news article now, actually faster than now. It needs to be over your by-line."

"And the subject is?" I asked.

"Joseph Monahan. We just took him from Leavenworth this morning and brought him here. Jack, what I'm telling you is Top Secret. We're sure that Monahan's got a target painted on his back. We found out that he was a senior guy in the planned attacks. We know it, but more importantly, al Qaeda knows it. So here's what your article will be about. Monahan was killed by a fellow prisoner, the name of which your source did not disclose. He was stabbed while returning to his cell after breakfast by a man with a make-shift knife. The reason for the article should be obvious to you. We want al Qaeda to think Monahan's dead so they don't try to kill him. He's secure here, but we don't want to take any chances at all."

"Buster, you're asking me to lie in a newspaper, and lie over my own by-line no less."

"No, Jack, I'm not *asking* you, Mr. Provisional CIA Agent, I'm *telling* you. I'm sure journalistic ethics includes a reporter doing everything possible to save his country when it's in danger. Monahan is valuable, to say the least. He's come over to our side and he's giving us an unbelievable amount of intelligence. We may have to take him on the road at some point. Keeping him safe is our highest priority. To make it easier on you, I will have two of my operatives corroborate the story, so you can console yourself that you checked additional sources."

Buster's a persuasive guy. His position, and mine as a provisional agent, puts him in a direct line of authority over me. If I refuse, he can probably have me arrested and locked up. But that's beside the point. He's right. This is no time for me to worry about protecting my reputation. If putting out misinformation gets us closer to a solution, I'll do it.

"Get me to a computer terminal, Buster."

><>< ><>

"Would-be Thanksgiving Bomber Killed in Prison"
Jack Thurber for *The Washington Times*

Joseph Monahan, one of the five American naval officers implicated in the plot to bomb American ships with nuclear weapons on Thanksgiving Day, has been killed. He was returning to his cell at Leavenworth prison after breakfast when he was attacked by an unknown man wielding a home-made knife.

Monahan was the weapons officer on the *USS Abraham Lincoln*. (full disclosure: Captain Ashley Patterson, the Commanding Officer of the *Lincoln*, is my wife).

The four other naval officers implicated in the Thanksgiving plot are Ralph Martin of the *USS Carl Vinson*, Philip Murphy of the *USS George Washington*, Frederick Peyton of the *USS Theodore Roosevelt*, and George Quentin of the *USS Harry Truman*.

A spokesman for the Central Intelligence Agency said he could not identify the killer at this point, and the CIA doesn't know if al Qaeda or any other terrorist organization was implicated.

Monahan is survived by his estranged wife, Janice Monahan, who had brought divorce proceedings. Efforts to get a statement from Mrs. Monahan were unsuccessful.

"Buster, this won't work."
"Why the hell not?"

"Everybody knows that I was supposed to be on the *USS Lincoln* on Thanksgiving Day. Anybody reading this will know that I'm not a disinterested reporter. I put in that 'full disclosure' bit to make it more believable, but I don't think the piece will accomplish what we want. Al Qaeda will smell a rat if they see my name."

"Okay," said Buster, "you have a point. Any ideas?"

"Simple," I said. "Wally Burton. He's here in Virginia on temporary assignment from *The New York Times*. As you know, he's also a provisional CIA agent. But you don't even have to ask Wally to lie. Just tell him the lie yourself and give him the contact information for the two operatives who will corroborate the story. Just tell him that Monahan was killed. To save time, you can give him the article I just wrote. He'll make his changes and file it immediately with the *Times*."

"Great thinking, Jack. You'd make a good spook."

Buster called Wally's office and sent him the story I wrote by encrypted email.

Wally rewrote the article, as would any good reporter. *The New York Times* piece reads:

"Would-be Bomber Joseph Monahan Killed in Prison"
Wallace Burton for *The New York Times*

Joseph Monahan, a former Lieutenant Commander in the United States Navy, and one of the five American naval officers implicated in the plot to bomb American ships with nuclear weapons on Thanksgiving Day, has been killed. He had been imprisoned at the high security prison at Leavenworth, Kansas. While was returning to his cell after breakfast he was attacked by an unknown man wielding a make-shift knife. He was dead upon arrival at the prison hospital.

Monahan was the weapons officer on the *USS Abraham Lincoln,* one of five American aircraft carriers that was targeted to be bombed on Thanksgiving Day, in a terrorist operation that has become known as the Thanksgiving Attacks.

The four other naval officers implicated in the Thanksgiving plot are Ralph Martin of the *USS Carl Vinson*, Philip Murphy of the *USS George Washington*, Frederick Peyton of the *USS Theodore Roosevelt*, and George Quentin of the *USS Harry Truman*.

A spokesman for the Central Intelligence Agency said he could not identify the killer at this point, and the CIA doesn't know if al Qaeda or any other terrorist organization was implicated. Calls to the FBI have not been returned, nor have attempts to contact the Office of Naval Intelligence.

Monahan is survived by his estranged wife, Janice Monahan, who had brought divorce proceedings. Efforts to get a statement from Mrs. Monahan were unsuccessful.

The story appeared within 20 minutes in the online version of the *Times*, and will be a headline in tomorrow's paper edition. Within minutes, all of the major networks and cable stations reported the story. As far as the world knows, Joe Monahan is a dead man.

CHAPTER THIRTY TWO

I can't believe that I'm about to meet with my soon-to-be ex-husband again. Admiral Frank thought it was essential that he speak to Joe in my presence, even though they had already met. Frank told me that because Joe is so important to the mission, he didn't want to take any chances that he may rethink anything. Frank believes my presence will help Joe get his mind centered. I don't get it, but who am I to argue with an admiral, especially a tall, good-looking one.

The interrogation room at the CIA was nicer than the one at Leavenworth. It was similar, but the furniture and flooring were much newer and more comfortable. I wonder if there's a course in architecture schools on designing interrogation rooms. *Make sure the gigantic one-way mirror is inconspicuous so the prisoner won't suspect it's a mirror.*

When Frank and I entered the room, Joe was already seated. His legs were shackled to the floor but his hands were free. As usual, I was feeling uncomfortable, so I figured I'd break the ice by asking Joe if he would like some coffee.

"Joe," said Frank, "I asked Janice to join us this afternoon, because she may be able to help you remember some things. I have no idea what they may be, but the human memory often needs some help."

"That's fine by me, Frank," Joe said. "I feel sad about what I did to this beautiful woman I lost, but it's great to see her again."

I guess I was supposed to comment on his remark. I said nothing

"Joe, Can you tell us about some of the participants in the plot, the people who work at the bomb plant?"

"Well, my memory is photographic when it comes to images, but to remember all the names of the al Qaeda operatives is a stretch. But that shouldn't be a problem. I'm sure the CIA has confiscated my computer. Have you looked at it?"

"Yes, we have," said Frank, "but there's nothing that we found that's in any way of interest to us. I saw that you were working on a novel, *An Oasis Too Far.* We had at least a dozen of our people look at what you wrote. It seems to be what it looks like, notes and drafts of a work of fiction."

"They showed it to me too, Joe," I said. "I had no idea you were working on a book, much less a novel. From the dates on the text files it seems that you were at it for a few years." (and it sucks, I thought).

"It's a lot more than a novel," Joe said. "it's a coded outline of the whole operation, most of which I've already told you about. But the most important information, based on what you asked me, is the Table of Characters."

"Table of Characters?" both Frank and I blurted out.

"Yup, there are about 45 characters in the book if I recall, with both Arabic and English names. The English names are fictitious, but the Arabic names are exactly what you're looking for. Start with the first character, then count down five and keep going. Every fifth name is one of the al Qaeda operatives involved in the upcoming attacks. If you bring me a printout of the names I'll identify them and give you background on each of them. Better yet, bring me the computer and I'll show you what else you missed."

Frank called his assistant, two floors above us. "Mike, bring Joseph Monahan's computer to room 0116."

——⟨+⟩——

Mike Smalley, Frank's aide, wheeled Joe's computer into the room on a cart. On the cart was also a small printer. Frank told him to put it on the table in front of Joe. We pulled our chairs to each side of him so we could follow what he was about to show us.

"Okay," said Joe, "here's the list of characters I told you about. Let's print it out and count off every five names. Next we're going to look at some stuff I think may be helpful. This page is entitled, as you can see, List of Code Names for the Sheik, he's the hero of the book."

"It just looks like a list of letters and numbers," I said.

"Yes, and when you read the codes backwards, you are looking at the license plate numbers of the key operatives. Frank, does this one look familiar?"

"Holy shit," Frank said, violating his self-imposed rule against cusswords, "that's *my* car."

"So it is, Sheik Abboud. You didn't think I'd leave you out did you?"

"Hold on," Frank said, "let's take a short break."

Frank walked over to the landline phone and picked it up.

"Buster, please come to room 0116 right now. You're not going to believe this."

CHAPTER THIRTY THREE

B uster walked into the room about two minutes after Frank called him.

"Buster, remember the novel on Joe's computer that we thought held no information for us? Well, it's more like a treasure trove."

Frank and I brought Buster up to date on what Joe had told us already, including the Table of Characters, and the license plates of the key al Qaeda players. Buster's eyes widened.

"I was about to show you the Table of Places and Scenes." said Joe. "You see this in a lot of novels. This is a list of addresses for safe houses that al Qaeda uses all over the country. It's a pretty simple code. Again, using the number five, this time as a divisor. If you see, for example 300 Norton Street, divide it by 5 and you get 60 Norton Street, which by the way is in Garden City, Long Island. It's been an al Qaeda safe house for about five years."

"Finally, this file looks like a word processing error, just a long string of numbers. These are cell phone numbers of all the key players, which I'm sure is out of date, but you may find it useful. The numbers are strung out in line after line, and each number is backwards."

Frank and Buster just looked at each other.

Buster, the man of action, stood up suddenly and said, "Okay, that's all I need for right now. I'm operating on two simple words. *Prepare* and *Act*, almost simultaneously. I'm going to take this data to my guys and have them start doing some fast police work. But before I go, I have a question. Do we have any bank account numbers in the book? They're great for tracking people down."

"That's one thing I don't have," said Joe. "I did handle banking assignments, but they change account numbers weekly."

"There's a guy I need to call," said Buster. "I don't know when he can get here, but I want another meeting as soon as he does."

"Oh, one last thing. Joe, do you consider *The New York Times* authoritative?"

"Well, sure."

"Good, then I regret to inform you that you're dead, killed at Leavenworth by an unknown assailant. *The New York Times* says so.

Frank and I couldn't help laughing. Buster moves at the speed of light.

Our meeting for the day was over, but my surprises weren't.

As we left the room, Frank touched my elbow and said, "Janice, can I have a word with you?"

"I'd ask you out for a drink if we weren't on lockdown, but could we just have a private chat in my office?"

My wise-cracking, smart-ass self almost said, "But I planned to watch *Dancing with the Stars* tonight."

What I said was, "Of course."

CHAPTER THIRTY FOUR

I loved Frank's office the moment I walked in. It exuded masculinity and power, but it also had a certain warmth to it. The emphasis was on leather, rich and sumptuous burgundy leather, which apparently was new because it let off a friendly, comforting smell. Frank, the country's most clandestine spy, did not advertise his recent exploits with photographs, just a few from his youth. He played football at Annapolis, and a few pictures of him in uniform adorned the walls.

"From this action shot, I'm guessing you were a running back," I said. "I can never understand how football players manage to pose for action shots. It looks like you're about to collapse in a heap after the photographer clicked the button."

"That's exactly what I did," Frank said. We both laughed.

"How about a drink, Janice?"

"That would be great. Just give me that bottle of vodka with straw and a slice of lemon."

"You've had a stressful few days, I take it."

"Try a few weeks, Frank. It seems like just yesterday that I went wormhole tripping with a known terrorist who turned out to be my road trip buddy."

Frank looked at me and smiled, a smile that said, "Yeah, I know what you mean." I hoped he was having a memory as pleasant as the one I had.

He poured vodka into a glass and some scotch for himself. He held my glass up and said, "Rocks?"

"That would be great, Honey."

Shit! "Honey?" What the hell was I saying. There's something about being subtle that I never seem to grasp. So I followed up my blatant flirtation by blubbering like a fool.

"Oh, gee, damn, I had no right to say that, I mean, I guess I'm tired from all of this stuff. I'm really sorry, Frank."

Frank brought our drinks over. He sat down next to me on the soft leather couch. He reached over and stroked my hand.

"That's okay, Janice. Actually I kind of liked the sound of it. 'Honey.' I can live with that."

"It's hard to believe that just a few days ago we were total strangers," I said. "I have a confession to make. I've checked you out. Once I found out that you were an admiral I realized that I knew even less about you than I thought."

"So how did you check me out?" Frank asked with a smile, still stroking my hand.

"I Googled your name, both your names, and read the entries into the early morning hours. I also asked people about you, especially Buster. In the last couple of days I've become an expert on Rear Admiral Frank Thompson. I feel like I've known you for a long time. So after our epic road trip and my hours of investigation, I've come to a conclusion."

"What's your conclusion?"

"You're a good man, a guy I'd like to be around more. A lot more. Did you do any research on me?" I asked.

"With the entire intelligence apparatus of the government at my disposal, what do you think?"

"I think I like you. A lot."

It was time for a kiss, but I'd been thinking that for quite a while. Frank seemed to think the same. He leaned over, looked at me with his gorgeous brown eyes, held my face in his left hand, and kissed me on the lips.

There are certain incidents in one's life that bring the world into focus. Stepping on a wormhole is like that. One minute you're here, the next you're in a different time. But a wormhole can't hold diddly-squat against a kiss from Frank Thompson.

"Honey, I've been meaning to have a chat with you for a long time," Frank said.

Honey, what a wonderful word. I hoped he wouldn't apologize to me for saying it. Honey? Cool. I'm his honey, and he's my honey. I'm feeling relaxed. I feel like I haven't felt this way in what seems an eternity. I feel calm, warm, happy, and I haven't even sipped my vodka yet.

"Yeah, me too," I said. I aspire to be articulate, but most of the time it's just an aspiration.

"I don't want to beat the obvious over the head with a baseball bat," said Frank, "but I think you'll agree that we, not to mention the whole country, are going through a strange and dangerous time. I just felt that I had to take a breather, sit down with you and let you know that I'm attracted to you. I really like you."

"Is that why you called me Honey?"

"Yes, Honey, it is."

Another kiss. A really long, make your eyes cloudy, tickle your nose, get the heart pumping kind of kiss.

Then I laughed. Actually, I cracked up.

"What's so funny, Honey?"

"I can't friggin believe that less than a week ago I sat in a car with a gun trained on you."

Frank laughed. "Can you guess when I really became attracted you, Janice?"

"I'm listening."

"I really started to like you when you pointed the gun away from me, put on the safety, and slipped it into your purse on the Jersey Turnpike."

"Men tell me that all the time," I said.

Frank looked adorable with Scotch squirting out of his nostrils. I jumped up and grabbed some tissues from his desk. Frank stood as we patted the Scotch dry on his suit. He continued to laugh and blow his nose.

He put both arms around my waist and pulled me close to him.

"I especially like a woman with a sense of humor."

We sat back down on the couch.

"Janice, since you're now a fellow spook, I have to bring you up to speed on some things, especially concerning me. I'm in lockdown. I live here at the CIA, and I'm not allowed to travel. There's a guy here who works in IT. He's a dead ringer for me, almost looks like he could be my twin. The Director has warned the guy to be careful. My lockdown is on direct orders from the White House. We know al Qaeda has a target on Joe Monahan's back, which is why he's here.

We also believe they're after me. I've been out of circulation for a while, my mole identity that is. As John le Carré would put it, I'm the spy who came in from the cold."

"I'll keep you warm," I said, as I wrapped my arms around his neck. What the hell. The two of us crossed a line and I wasn't about to go back.

Another kiss. I won't even describe this one. I want to keep it to myself. Deep breath.

"So I can't even leave the CIA compound until the mission is over."

"So you have, uh, like a room right here at the Agency?"

"Yes, it's really a well-furnished apartment, right here on campus."

"And you're actually able to, like, uh, entertain guests?" I figured I'd go where we both wanted to go.

"Well, the Agency has all kinds of rules, but when you hit a certain level of seniority, the rules bend a bit."

"So why don't we bend the rules a bit?"

As I've said, subtlety is not my strong suit.

Frank leaned over and kissed me, again.

"I hope I'm not being too forward," said Frank.

"Forward?" I said. "What makes you think you're being forward?"

"Well," said Frank, "This is, after all, our first date."

"What do you mean our first date?" I asked. "This is our fifth date."

"What?" said Frank. "How is this our fifth date?"

"Let's count them," I said. "Our first date was when we came through the wormhole. Our second was when I bought you a hot dog at the food stand in Manhattan after you threw up. Our third date was at the car rental office. Then came our fourth date at the Vince Lombardi Service area on the New Jersey Turnpike. That's when I put the gun in my purse. And finally, we're on our fifth date, right here."

"Well then," said Frank, "allow me to invite you on our sixth date, at my apartment. I think it's fair to say that I like you – a lot."

"Does that explain why your hand is under my skirt?"

CHAPTER THIRTY FIVE

The private residences at the CIA are impressive, although not to be confused with the Waldorf. The hallways and common areas have an almost pleasant atmosphere, a place where temporarily assigned spies can feel at home, if only for a little while. I felt intimidated about walking past Frank's bodyguards on our way to his apartment, but Frank assured me that these were two trusted guys, with a strong sense of discretion. Hell, he's not married so why should they care? Because I wasn't sure where Mother Agency would be sending me that night, I carried a bag packed with a change of clothes.

Frank's apartment impressed me almost as much as his office. Not as much leather, but it was, as he said, well-furnished. My engineer's eye sized it up to be about 1,250 square feet. It boasted an eat-in kitchen, two full bathrooms and two bedrooms, one of which was totally unnecessary, I thought. (Chill, stop, move slow, be cool).

We never did get to our drinks at Frank's office, so he poured us two more, making sure to serve my drink with his right hand, and giving me a cocktail napkin without me having to ask. How can this guy be so urbane and charming when he's spent part of his life spooking around the world's hell holes?

Frank gave me a quick tour of the apartment, which, at 1,250 square feet went quickly. All the while we held hands, which was fine with me.

"So how do you keep such a beautiful figure?" asked Frank, being totally flirtatious, which was also fine with me.

"I'm a fitness nut. How about you, Handsome?"

"I burn a lot of calories chasing things and running away from things."

We both agreed that we felt kind of grungy after yet another day of meetings. I was a little nervous that Frank would crack one of those lame "why don't we conserve water" jokes. Things are moving fast, but just fast enough. I felt relieved when he said that I'd find a fresh robe hanging on the guest bath door.

The shower, as showers always do, felt great. He even supplied my favorite bar soap. Maybe he found this out when he ran his intelligence report on me. The white terry robe hanging on the door was emblazoned with "United States Naval Academy," and a "Beat Army" patch on the sleeve. I guess Admiral Frank, CIA spook on loan, likes to remind himself that he's still employed by the United States Navy. I briefly wondered why the guest bathrobe. Has he had guests there before? None of my business, I concluded, as long as she stays the hell away from now on. Stop being childish. It's time to come out and play.

I put on the robe. The bottom of it cascaded to a puddle of fabric four inches deep. The shoulders began at my elbows. At 5'10," I'm not short, but this robe fit me like a blanket. I fantasized about my Snow White moment, but I looked like Dopey the Dwarf.

I walked into the living room, hiking up my regal bathrobe so as not to trip and fall on my face. Frank was pouring us drinks. He looked at me and laughed.

"What's so amusing?" I asked, looking like a poorly wrapped sandwich.

"That robe was given to me as a joke gift at an Army-Navy Game. A guy on stilts wore it in the half-time parade. But you look beautiful anyway."

He sat on the couch and I sat next to him, with my face nestled on his shoulder.

It may sound crazy, but he seemed a little nervous. Maybe it's been a long time. It sure as hell had been for me. This is going to be clumsy, I thought, and fun.

Frank couldn't seem to find words beyond small talk, and I found this cute as hell. I held his handsome face in my hands and said, "Hey sailor, I thought you were going to show me your art work."

We walked into the master bedroom and faced each other at the foot of the bed. I dropped my gigantic United States Naval Academy robe to the floor. Frank did the same with his.

Frank then showed me his art work, and what wonderful, breathtaking art it was. What a talented artist. "That one's great. Wait, wait, show me that again. Oh my God, what an artist, just keep on, on, on, uh, showing me."

In the woozy, cozy afterglow of our lovemaking we lay still. Some feelings you don't want go away. You just try to recreate them and keep them part of you. That's how I felt. I love this man. Okay, I only met him a few days ago, but I've learned all about him, and he's learned everything about me. I'm not just attracted to him, I love him. In all of the crazy shit I've gone through in the past three weeks I've learned what I want and what I don't want. Him, I want.

I rolled on top of him, and immediately felt that he was ready for more. I held his face in my hands and said the simple words, "I love you."

"Say that again, Janice."

"I love you."

"My turn. I love you."

We embraced for so long I thought we went through another wormhole.

"What's next for us, Frank?" I said as I stared into his eyes.

"Honey, after this thing is over, and it will be over because we're gonna win it, you and I have a lifetime to figure out what's next."

"A lifetime?"

"You heard me."

Fate can be strange. Sometimes you think it's on your side, other times not. A short while ago I was on a road trip with a man who frightened and confused me. Now, I am drop dead, head over heels in love with him, and I think my feelings are reciprocated.

I've noticed something about time travelers, including Frank and me.

We don't like to waste time.

CHAPTER THIRTY SIX

This morning's headline in *The New York Times* reads, "Thanksgiving Bomber Joseph Monahan Killed in Prison."

"Sheik Haddad, have you seen the newspaper, sir?" said Hussein Basara, aide to Sheik Abbas Haddad.

"Yes, and I think it's an infidel lie. The report does not say who the killer was but leaves the impression that it may have been a targeted assassination. As we know, that's impossible because I am the only one who could have ordered such an action. No, I believe the infidels have planted this story to convince us that Monahan is dead, to stop our plans to kill him."

"But Sheik Haddad, if I may sir, these American newspapers, especially important ones like *The New York Times*, only go to print when the information has been checked with other sources, usually at least two."

"Hussein, my brother, are you so naive as to think that someone could not have simply planted the 'sources'? I think that the Americans are trying to fool us into believing that Monahan is dead.

Put out the word to all of our contacts to look and listen for any information about Monahan. I believe he lives. He *must* be killed."

"And what about Ayham Abboud, sir? Has there still been no contact with him?"

"No, there has not. This is a mystery to me. If the Americans have captured him they know how valuable he is, and what's more important, they know that *we* know his value. But there have been no newspaper reports about Sheik Abboud at all. And naturally, without any evidence people begin to speculate, including our own brothers. I even heard a ridiculous rumor yesterday that Ayham Abboud is really an American Navy admiral."

Basara laughed so hard he spilled his tea.

"It's good to see you laugh, my brother. We must laugh when we hear nonsense. Can you imagine, Sheik Abboud an admiral?"

They both laughed.

"But laughter cannot replace vigilance," said Haddad. "Until we know the fate of Sheik Abboud, we must assume the worst, that he is in American custody."

CHAPTER THIRTY SEVEN

The good old Thanksgiving Gang has been called to Director Bill Carlini's office at the CIA. Old Thanksgiving Gang? I can't believe I thought that. Old? About three weeks ago I was a quiet HVAC engineer designing an air conditioning system for a bank in New Jersey. I had never heard of The Thanksgiving Gang, because it didn't exist. *Three weeks ago.*

⊨⊨ ⊫⊫

Director Bill Carlini called the meeting to order. Carlini's a good man. In the midst of all this madness, it's comforting having a smart, level-headed guy in charge. The Thanksgiving Gang was there: Jack Thurber, Bennie Weinberg, Wally Burton, myself, and of course, our gang leader, CIA Agent Buster. I had hoped that Jack's wife Ashley, my new friend, would be there, but she has this little detail in her life called running a nuclear aircraft carrier. Non-gang members included my soon-to-be ex-husband Joe Monahan, to whom I no longer refer to as *scumbag,* and Admiral Frank Thompson, aka Ayham Abboud, aka Frankie of Arabia, aka the-man-I-love. Those last two "aka's" were left out of Carlini's introductions.

Joe Monahan's legs were shackled to the floor, which we all thought was silly, but apparently there's a strict CIA protocol when prisoners attend meetings.

"Folks," said Carlini, "I'm going to turn this meeting over to Buster. He's not only the best agent in the CIA, he's the best agent I could ever imagine. I don't have a lot of say in the matter, but I've already recommended to the White House that Buster take over my job when I retire."

"Thank you Mr. Director, and thank you for your kind words," said Buster. "Folks, you've heard me say it before, but I'll repeat it. This operation, unfortunately, involves a lot of meetings, because there's so much information we need to get our hands on. But the two watchwords we all need to keep in mind are *Prepare* and *Act*. Sounds logical enough, I know, but the difference here is that the *Prepare* and *Act* details need to be done almost simultaneously because we have so little time. For example, Joe Monahan here has given us excellent information from his computer, information that we didn't see, but information that he interpreted for us. He's given us the names of all of the al Qaeda operatives, including some minor players. We also found the license plate numbers of all the major players. One of the best lists Joe has given us are the locations of al Qaeda safe houses across the country. So that was the *Prepare* part. Before Joe was done speaking I gave those lists to our people here at the Agency, and they've been working at it all night. That's the *Act* part. Basic police work, yes. And basic police work is what usually solves crimes."

"Buster, if I may," said Jack Thurber, himself a no-slouch investigator. "Besides these lists, and besides what will happen when we work the lists, is there anything we're missing?"

"Jack, it's almost like you and I rehearsed this, because I was just about to get to that point. The only thing we're missing is banking information, cash flow, and stuff like that. Tracing money is often a spy's best way to get to a destination. So to help us with that part of the puzzle, we have a special guest."

CHAPTER THIRTY EIGHT

A guard opened the door and in strode a tall Middle Eastern-looking man carrying a briefcase and dressed in the most expensive Savile Row suit I'd ever seen.

"G'day, Mates," said the man in an Australian accent.

"Trevor!" the gang shouted in unison.

We all got off our seats and stormed Trevor as if he were a rock star. When you see an old friend, especially a friend you thought was dead, tears flow. I was happy that I wasn't alone, indulging in a "girlie" thing, because I noticed that Jack, Ben and Wally were wiping tears away as well. We all loved Trevor, for reasons that will be obvious shortly.

After we took our seats, and before he was introduced to the others, I asked Trevor, "How the hell did you get here?"

Before Trevor could answer, Buster frowned and gave me one of his "you don't have a need to know" looks.

"For the couple of folks here that don't know him," Buster said, "Trevor McMartin is a bank examiner, a man who traces down money. He's from Australia in case you hadn't noticed, even though he looks like he could be from either my family or Admiral Frank's. His Lebanese name is Salem Yousef."

Buster's right. He, Trevor, and Frank all have their familial Middle Eastern appearances, although Frank is by far the best looking by a desert mile. (But I digress.)

"Trevor was enormously helpful to us when we were trying to find the whereabouts of Joe Monahan and his former friends. We've tracked down Trevor's background, which I'm sure comes as no surprise to him." Buster turned to Trevor, who smiled and nodded. "He's like a one-man IRS and FBI combined. Trevor is to money like a bloodhound is to a scent."

"Nice way of puttin' it, Matey."

"I contacted Trevor last night. By stroke of luck he was in DC on assignment so he was able to come to this meeting. Trevor's worked for the United States Government over the years and holds a Top Secret security clearance, so, with his agreement, we've hired him. We may have to put a special line in the budget because Trevor makes a ton of dough for his work."

"No worry, Mate. Given the circumstance you described I consider this my patriotic duty as an Aussie and friend of your great country."

"Just to remind everybody," said Buster, "in all of this complicated operation we have one objective, and that objective isn't complicated. We've got to find the bombs. Trevor, please give us a few words, and please remember the *need to know* rule about the details."

"Buster over here (*Busta ova heah*) gave me a bit of information last night. I know I can't go in depth on details, but I just want you folks to know that I already have some solid leads based on tracking I've been doing even before I got the word from Buster. Believe it or not, even though I just learned about this last night, I have a strong hunch where the bombs may be, based on some active banking transactions. I can't go further into that because Buster's right: *Need to know* is an important part of security. Even the best-intentioned people can blurt things out. If you don't have the knowledge you've got nothing to blurt. Buster's the boss, and he'll share knowledge when necessary. Now if you blokes will pardon me, I've got a lot of work to do."

CHAPTER THIRTY NINE

Buster here.

Today's Monday, October 26, 2015, a month from Thanksgiving Day. I'm trying to drive events as fast as I can. On Jack Thurber's suggestion I've been putting in at least a half-hour of aerobic exercise every day to keep my head clear, and my stomach from yelling at me.

I'm at Director Carlini's office with our Australian friend, Trevor McMartin. Trevor's one of the smartest and smoothest operators I've ever seen in action. I'd love to recruit him to the Agency but we couldn't come close to matching the money he makes.

This meeting will consist of me, Director Carlini, and Trevor. As any spook knows, it's essential to limit the amount of people who have knowledge of the details of any operation. My Thanksgiving Gang friends are the most trustworthy people I've ever met and I'd put my life in their hands. But, the fewer the people who know of a secret, the more chance the secret has of remaining just that, a secret.

Director Carlini walked in.

"Mr. McMartin, a pleasure to meet you, sir. Your reputation is way out in front of you. Buster tells me that you're already focusing in on the question of the century – where are the bombs?"

"Mr. Director, yes, I am starting to focus on something, but don't get too excited yet. I don't have to tell you folks that a promising lead often goes nowhere. I'm in the business of chasing money. To me, money is like an animal. To chase it you have to know what it wants. If you want to find monkeys, look for the banana trees. So I look first to where the money is going and then try to answer the question why."

"Trevor, if you don't mind me asking," said Carlini, "do you work from intuition based on experience, or do you have a more objective way of analysis."

"It's all in the numbers, Mr. Director. To answer your question, yes I try to be completely objective. Intuition from years of experience plays a part, but only a part. I've designed a computer algorithm that knows how to chase money. Without boring you with the details, my algorithm looks at flows of assets and then tracks the assets. It also has built in a long string of possible reasons why the assets are going where they're going. For example, if a car manufacturer is setting up a new plant in a new city, the algorithm takes this into account, be-cause the program expects to see a lot of money coming and going to various subcontractors. The result is a bunch of patterns, sometimes not clear, but often they jump off the page at you. I may have found a page jumper. Look here."

Trevor then laid out for us three sheets of paper with both bar and line graphs. On three other pieces of paper were odd-looking cluster graphs. I couldn't tell exactly what these graphs meant, but right away I saw some concentrated patterns. I pointed them out to the Director and he saw the same thing. Carlini, with a math degree from Stamford, is no amateur when it comes to technical matters.

"Trevor," I said. "I think the Director and I both see some definite patterns. Can you summarize it for us?"

"Denver, Colorado, mates."

Carlini and I looked at one another.

"Please explain, Trevor."

"There's been a lot of money going in and out of Denver banks in the last few months. I even checked to see if a new casino had been built. Actually, that kind of data is programmed into my algorithm. Some of the money has been spent on real estate, and a lot on construction. But there's also been a lot of dollars spent on technical equipment and security devices."

"Can you tell where the money comes from?" I asked.

"Various parts of the Middle East, a lot from Saudi Arabia, and a good bit from Yemen."

"I find it hard to believe that you possess this information, if you don't mind me saying, Trevor," said Carlini. "Frankly I wasn't aware that it was legal."

"Mate, if some other bloke with a good head for math tried to do what I do he'd be in prison. I'm well known to governments around the world and I do a lot of business with them. Just ask your State Department. Those fellas know me well."

Carlini looked at me.

"I did, and they do," I said. "Trevor, you amaze me."

I called my assistant Phil Lopez. Trevor had given us a location, a possible location to focus on. We also had Joe Monahan's drawing of the site to work with. Monahan didn't know where it was, but now we had another dot to connect. The sketch had already been plugged into a computer digitally so now it's a question of satellite scanning to find something that matches the sketch, narrowed to Denver, Colorado.

Just before noon my assistant called and screamed, yes screamed, "Buster, you have got to fucking see this!'

A minute later Phil came running into the room, apologizing to Carlini for the intrusion. Carlini didn't mind; he wanted results. A quick glance at what Phil Lopez put on the table showed us photographs, amazing photographs.

I called the lockup unit and told the guard to bring Joe Monahan to the Director's office.

In a few minutes, Monahan came clattering in to the office dragging his leg irons and being led by two guards. Trevor, who had once photographed Monahan in Yemen going into a bank, regarded him through squinted eye lids.

"Joe, what do you think?" I said, gesturing to the printout that Lopez had put on the table. "Show us your photographic memory talents."

"That's it, Buster, that's it! You're looking at the exact location I've seen before from aerial photos. Where is it?"

"Sorry, Mr. Monahan," said Carlini, "but you don't need to know that."

"Buster, let's get the group here now."

I speed dialed Jack Thurber, Wally Burton, Bennie, Janice, and Admiral Frank. Everyone knew to expect a call at any moment during this operation, so they all showed up within 10 minutes.

CHAPTER FORTY

J anice here.

Another meeting, but it's to be expected. I'm still thinking about my meeting last night with Frank. I doubt this one will be as interesting. Frank and I arrived five minutes apart. Nothing wrong with a little discretion.

We all took our seats around the table in a pecking order that seemed to have evolved. I sat next to Frank. Why not?

"Okay, everybody," said Carlini, "we are now halfway there, more than halfway. We've found the bomb plant."

He let that sink in. My God, we've found the bombs.

"Buster?" Carlini gestured to his favorite spook.

"As the Director has just pointed out," said Buster, "we're halfway there. Thanks to Joe Monahan's photographic memory and Janice's engineering drawing skills, we've located the bomb plant. So, my friends, the next question is on the table – now what? We already know that we can't go in guns blazing around nuclear weapons. We need to find an answer, now."

"Gas," I said.

Everyone looked at me with confusion on their faces, like I just requested some Tums.

"Yes, gas. I don't know what kind of weapons the military stockpiles, but I'm thinking either a lethal or non-lethal gas. All we have to figure out is how to get it into the building. I'm guessing some kind of robotic tunneling device. I can design the piping. I know how to deliver air conditioning to large buildings. I'm sure I can deliver gas in the same way."

Buster jumped up, ran around the table and kissed me on the forehead, then ran out of the room, to make a string of phone calls I'm sure.

"Janice, you've obviously nailed it on the head," said Carlini. "I expect Buster back in a few minutes to let us know that the plans are on the way."

"Mr. Director," said Wally Burton, "I wrote an article a couple of years ago about the chemical weapons the United States stockpiles. Everyone I interviewed said that the chemicals are for studying defensive procedures, to get to know an enemy's capabilities in case the weapons are used against us. Among the nasty stuff we stockpile is nerve gas. A dose of that could knock out a building full of people."

"Hold on folks," said Frank. "I think Director Carlini will agree that the use of a lethal chemical weapon is against national policy. Yes, we're faced with an emergency, and the ultimate decision will come from the White House, but my thinking is that we should use a non-lethal debilitating agent. Janice, your thoughts?"

With that Frank put his hand under the table and squeezed my knee. Interesting way to get information out of me I thought, but I didn't complain.

"I'm not an expert on gasses," I said, "but I do know a bit about delivery of air, both cold and hot. From my general reading, I've learned that CS gas, also known as common tear gas, is a powerful debilitating agent. As we all know from just watching TV, it's usually delivered by a type of hand grenade or artillery shell. The thing explodes just enough to release the gas and the intended recipients scatter, choking and teary eyed. The gas constricts breathing and can immobilize a person in seconds. Correct me if I'm wrong, but tear gas is normally used outdoors. If we have a large enough pipe, I'm thinking two to three inches in diameter, and a strong enough mechanical blower, we could secure a building full of people in moments. The building that we just saw in the satellite photographs is only one story tall, a perfect target. We just need to figure out how to tunnel under the building and then tunnel up through the floor. Buster's probably got that figured out already."

CHAPTER FORTY ONE

An alarm rang through the building, interrupting our meeting. At the same time, two armed Marines ran into the office, their carbines held down at a 45-degree angle.

"There's been a shooting in front of the building, Sir," said one of the Marines. "I've been ordered to request that you remain in this room."

We could hear the sound of boots as Marines ran through the building to take defensive positions.

Because all of the big news networks have assigned full-time reporters at the CIA, the word went out fast.

Carlini clicked on an array of TVs on a wall behind our meeting table and then clicked the volume on CNN, which was reporting the incident.

"There has been a shooting in broad daylight in front of the Central Intelligence Agency," the CNN reporter said. "The incident happened just a few minutes ago at 12:15 PM Eastern Time. We have confirmed that the victim, whose family has been notified, is Jerome Bradley, a computer programmer at the CIA. He was on his way to lunch when he was shot. Security personnel gunned down and killed the shooter immediately. The identity of the gunman is unknown at this point, but he's reported to be a man in his 20s of Middle Eastern appearance. We have no information as to motive or whether the shooting was terror related. According to protocol, the Central Intelligence Agency is in lockdown until further notice."

—•— —•—

Director Carlini looked at Frank and said, "Jerry Bradley was your look-alike, Frank, the guy everybody kept confusing with you."

I looked at Frank and his words about being under personal lockdown came back to me. *The spy who came in from the cold* like hell. The cold has followed him here. Somebody's out to kill Frank, *my* Frank. I patted my waist and felt a bit of comfort that my Glock was in place.

Director Carlini had recently ordered that all agents, regular and deputy, carry weapons at all times.

"I'm doubling your security detail, Frank, and not just at your residence. Wherever you go there will be two armed guards with you." And I'll be the third, I thought.

"Let's think this through, Mr. Director," said Frank. "If this was an attempted hit on me, and at this point it appears that it was, it tells us that al Qaeda knew I was here. Up until now they just thought I was missing. Somebody leaked this from inside, and whoever did probably has leaked Joe Monahan's presence as well. I recommend we double Monahan's security."

A knock on the door caused us all to feel for our side arms. One of our Marine guards opened it and someone handed him a piece of paper. He brought it to Carlini.

"Take a look at this, Frank. It's a photo of the shooter."

"Abdul Kabani," said Frank, "an al Qaeda operative. The last time I saw him was in Yemen."

Carlini picked up the phone. "The name is Abdul Kabani. He's with al Qaeda, last seen in Yemen. Do a National Agency Check as well as FBI and Europol rundowns and let me know whatever you find out about him."

"What's obvious to me," said Bennie, "is that these guys are getting desperate. To put a known al Qaeda operative on an assassination job in broad daylight tells me that they're really nervous."

"It looks like a second front just opened," said Carlini. "Janice, Jack, Ben, and Wally, please make arrangements to move here to the Agency temporarily. We have plenty of residences. You'll be comfortable, but most of all, secure."

No problem, I already have a place, I almost said.

"Frank," said Carlini, "as soon as we're able to move around the building I want you to report to the clandestine ops people for a makeover. The last damn thing I want to see or read is that there's a man at CIA who bears a resemblance to Jerome Bradley, the poor guy who was shot. The next time I see you, please introduce yourself because I won't recognize you."

"Okay everybody, quick break while we wait for Buster. Don't go far, because you won't get far. We're still on lockdown."

CHAPTER FORTY TWO

Everybody filed out of the room. Frank and I stood in a small anteroom next to the conference space.

"I will torture, maim, and dismember anyone who so much as lays a hand on you, Frank."

Frank put a hand on my waist and pulled me closer to him.

"Listen, tough lady, and please listen carefully. When things get dicey, and they always get dicey in this business, the last emotions you want are anger and hatred. Fear will take care of itself, but anger and hatred are your worst enemies. They cloud your decisions and cause you to make the wrong moves. Think of the mission, only the mission. Our job isn't to hate the bad guys; our job is to kill them."

"Okay, then I'll just kill them."

Frank laughed. Then I laughed. I can't believe we're laughing. Maybe I'm turning into a hardened spook. Frank made a good point about keeping emotions in check. Think mission. Good advice. So I'll just feel sorry for the man who lays a finger on my Frankie. We were still alone so we took the opportunity for a hug. After the shooting I didn't want to stop hugging him. Then he put both hands on my butt. Suddenly he pulled them away.

"Hey, I didn't tell you to stop that."

"The others are returning to the room, Honey."

Just enough time for a quick kiss.

━┿ ┿━

Buster, everybody's favorite man of action, walked back into the room.

"That shooting that just happened tells us that we have to move fast. Obviously you folks have been talking about just that while I was upstairs. I've taken Janice's ideas about tear gas and chased down the possibilities. This can work. My guy at the Pentagon, well one of my guys at the Pentagon, told me about a small-fast moving robot that they use for tunneling. It can dig a tunnel up to three inches in diameter, just what Janice was looking for. It's controlled by powerful remote telemetry, so we can give it commands while it's deep under dirt. When it makes its turn and hits the bottom of the building, it quietly screws a small opening and surveys the room with a camera, giving us a real-time view of what's going on. Then it will bore the larger hole through the concrete to connect the gas pipe, which it will drag behind it. A powerful fan, the kind they use in aircraft simulators, will blow the tear gas directly through the pipe, pushing a large volume of gas right into the building. There will be a lot of tear gas, a whole lot more than the stuff you see dispersing crowds on TV. And remember, this will happen inside a structure so the punch will be much more powerful. Any personnel inside the building will be immobilized within seconds."

"How soon can we start digging, Buster?" asked the Director.

"We've started already."

CHAPTER FORTY THREE

B uster tasked me to work on the connector between the blower and the end of the pipe. This was actually easy, but Buster being Buster, he wanted me to move into a temporary office right next to his so that we could work faster. Buster moves so fast he almost disappears in front of your eyes. Today is Tuesday, October 27, less than a month to Thanksgiving Day, so nobody complained about Buster's speed and crankiness.

As I walked down a hallway to my new office, an interesting looking man walked toward me. He had a long white beard, rimless glasses, and wore a floppy hat. The man looked like an Oxford professor. This guy can stand to lose some weight, I thought, looking at his huge gut. He wore baggy blue jeans, old fashioned sneakers, and a frumpy sweatshirt.

"Hello," I said politely as I walked past him, concentrating on my design task.

"Good morning, Honey," said the man in a familiar deep baritone voice.

I know that voice from somewhere, I thought, and who the hell is he to call me honey?

"Dinner tonight?" he then said.

I turned and looked at him, as he turned and looked at me. I didn't know whether to laugh, cry, or scream.

"Frankie!" I said, putting my hands over my mouth and trying to keep my voice down.

"What have they done to you?"

"Those clandestine ops people have a weird sense of humor, I'm afraid," said Frank.

I was laughing so hard, tears started to stream down my face. Buster turned the corner, saw my tear drenched face, and put on a hard look.

Buster put both hands on his hips and flashed a face that said, "Don't mess with my agent."

"My name is Agent Gamal Akhbar, and you would be?"

"Hey, pal, I outrank you. Mind if I call you Buster?"

Buster cracked up. "Those clan ops people have done a few numbers on me over the years, but nothing like this. Do we still call you Frank?"

"No, the Director wants me to be Professor Michael Reynolds, a consultant from Virginia Tech."

"Welcome to the Agency, Professor Mike." Buster continued toward his office, still laughing.

I knew I should follow immediately because Buster gets in a raggedy mood if anyone's late for a meeting.

I gave Professor Mike a quick kiss through his tickly fake beard, and patted his "stomach."

"Later, Honey," Frank said.

I cracked up laughing again.

CHAPTER FORTY FOUR

"Sheik Haddad, I'm so sorry for the troubling news from Virginia," said Hussein Basara, Haddad's assistant.

"It's obvious that Ayham Abboud has been co-opted by the infidels, brother Basara, otherwise they would never have planted a lookalike at the CIA. Sadly, brother Kabani was killed in the operation, but he is now in heaven receiving his reward. Sheik Abboud is still missing, as is Abu Hussein, the man the infidels call Monahan. I have read the news reports that Monahan was killed in prison, but I still don't believe them."

"Today is October 27, my brother. Are the weapons for our quest ready to use?"

"Yes, sir, the timing devices have been inserted, and they await arming at your command."

"The day approaches, brother Basara. But we still must keep all of our senses opened to the whereabouts of Monahan and Sheik Abboud."

"Should we not calm ourselves my Sheik? The one thing that they cannot know is our alternate plan. They can't know it because neither Monahan or Abboud know it."

"You are right my brother. Our plans cannot be stopped this time."

CHAPTER FORTY FIVE

Today is October 28. We'd just delivered 500 feet of flexible plastic piping to a building in Denver, next door to our target. Buster ordered the building to be rented four days before. We only needed about 275 feet of pipe, but Buster likes to build in safety margins. The tunneling began and, according to Buster, the robot would be ready to penetrate the building at 7 PM Eastern time. After an operation like this I don't think I'll ever look at another HVAC project in the same way. I'd checked and rechecked the blower system that will force the tear gas into the building. It's so powerful it can almost blow over a minivan, which is exactly what we did in our testing.

The tension around here was getting severe. Our meetings usually include a few moments of levity and some ice-breaking laughter. That hadn't been happening. The only good laugh I had recently was at Frank's crazy new costume.

I'm going to hit the gym for a workout. Later I'll take a nap. I want to be in the conference room at 7 PM. Carlini said he would show a real-time video of the operation.

As fate would have it, or maybe it's just dumb luck, the apartment the CIA assigned me is just down the hall from Frank. Maybe I'll see him later and stroke his new beard, or fiddle with his tummy pillow or, well, we'll think of something.

CHAPTER FORTY SIX

I t's less than a month to Thanksgiving. I'm glad I had my workout and a nap. With the Thanksgiving Attacks less than a month away, the tension was so tight you could hear music if you plucked at the air. We all gathered in Director Carlini's office for a live video feed of our tunneling operation. A tray of finger sandwiches and light snacks was placed in the corner of the room, but nobody even bothered to take the cellophane wrap off the tray. This was a command performance, and yours truly was the symphony director, giving my stomach a knot that I didn't know where to locate.

The time was 6:45 PM, fifteen minutes to our expected breakthrough into the building. The first pipe will emerge in a corner of the large building, and the second will pop up through the bomb room itself. As designed, the first piece of equipment to emerge is a small shaft with a camera and microphone attached to the top.

A Navy SEAL unit of 12 men was poised inside the building next door, fully armed and armored, ready to raid the building as soon as the tear gas was released. Each SEAL wore an OBA or oxygen breathing apparatus. Any person in the building who wasn't incapacitated by the tear gas would soon be stunned by the SEALs.

Pipe unit one emerged through the floor in the main room as planned. It was a quarter-inch in diameter and drilled up through the floor silently. There was no sound in Carlini's office either. The shaft, along with its camera and microphone, rotated 360 degrees for a full view of the larger room. The lights were on but we couldn't see anyone, not one person.

The second unit poked its shaft up through the floor in the bomb room. The space was also well-lit. Not one man appeared in view.

"Maybe they're outside having a smoke," said Buster, his voice uncharacteristically high pitched.

He switched to the live satellite feed so we could observe the outside of the building. As always, the perimeter was flooded with light. A squirrel darted across the screen, the only evidence of life at the Denver bomb plant.

"Let's have a better look at the bomb room," said Buster after he took a swig of water. I've never seen Buster look so nervous.

The operator raised the camera shaft to full height, showing us the table with the suitcase bombs.

The suitcases were all open.

They were all empty.

CHAPTER FORTY SEVEN

Sometimes words fail when they're needed the most. Throughout history, stirring words have come to the rescue when a situation looked dire. "Damn the torpedoes, full speed ahead." "Don't shoot till you see the whites of their eyes." "Away all boats." The right word at the right time saves the day.

But there weren't *any* words to capture the mood in the office. The room was as silent as the empty bomb building we just saw.

Obviously, the ball was in Carlini's court. He was the top official in the room, and we all expected him to say something to make the situation less tense, less frightening.

"Folks," said Carlini, "we don't get paid to wallow in disappointment. We get paid to move forward and make things happen. We've just been dealt a bad hand. Time to reshuffle and play on."

Not exactly General Patton, I thought, but pretty good for the circumstances. The best part about his words was that they played right into the hands of Mr. Action Man himself, Buster.

"Phil," Buster shouted to his aide over the phone, "Find Trevor McMartin and bring him to the Director's office immediately."

⟞⟨⟩⟝

The ever elegant Trevor walked into the room, a briefcase in one hand.

"I was about to say G'day, mates, but the looks on your faces tell me this hasn't been a good day."

"Here's the Denver bomb plant, Trevor," said Buster pointing the still images of the empty rooms, and lingering on the empty suitcases.

"Trevor, we're back to the starting line," said Buster.

CHAPTER FORTY EIGHT

The Sea Bounder, a 512-foot freighter, was stopped in the calm Atlantic waters off New York's Long Island. It was 8:45 PM on the evening of October 28, 2015. The night was dark as black ink, with no stars or moon, ideal conditions for a sensitive transfer operation in the ocean.

Captain Woody Bouchard, the skipper of *The Sea Bounder*, smiled broadly as he stood on a lower cargo platform along with three of his crewmen. Bouchard, a 51-year-old Canadian, smiled because he was about to come into a large amount of cash. The operation was a simple one, merely transfer some packages to a nearby vessel. The captain had done this hundreds of times, although seldom was there so much money involved. In a time of advanced cyber crime and Internet fraud, Bouchard was a simple man, a throwback to a simpler time. He was an old-fashioned smuggler, and a skilled one. He fancied himself a professional, and even studied the history of his craft. Long Island, Bouchard recalled, played a prominent role in bootlegging during Prohibition. Ships like his, back in the 1920s, would often engage in operations similar to tonight's venture. A freighter would come to a stop off the South Shore of Long Island and would be greeted by smaller and faster boats that would take the cases of bootleg liquor and enter the Great South Bay through the Fire Island Inlet. Once in the bay the small boats would proceed to a designated pier and make a quick rendezvous with smugglers ashore who would bring the booze to speakeasies around Long Island and the New York Metropolitan area. It's still done today, but the cargo is drugs, not liquor, and the smaller vessels are usually powerful Cigarette boats. Knowledgeable Long Islanders, hearing the powerful roar of a Cigarette boat in the early morning hours, assume that a drug drop is in the works.

Woody Bouchard is popular with the people he does business with because he never asks questions. He just makes the deliveries.

Although the sea was calm, Bouchard maneuvered *The Sea Bounder* to create a *lee* on the starboard side, an area of calm caused by the freighter's bulk against the waves on the other side of the ship. As Bouchard and his crewmen stood on the loading platform on the starboard side, a sleek multimillion dollar 85-foot yacht pulled up to the platform. The man operating the yacht guided it next to the ship, where heavy rubber fenders were strung to protect it from damage. The yacht bore the name *Andiamo*. Bouchard smiled at the name. *Andiamo*, "Let's Go," in Italian.

When *Andiamo* was secured alongside the freighter, a man stepped up onto the platform, along with two of his colleagues.

"Captain Woody Bouchard at your service, sir. And with whom do I have the pleasure?"

"I am Mr. Jones (*Meester Jones*)," said the man in a heavy Middle Eastern accent.

"My pleasure, Mr. Jones," said Bouchard. "Let's first attend to business if you don't mind."

Mr. Jones swung a suitcase from the yacht to the platform. Bouchard opened it and counted the cash, something he knew how to do quickly. One million American dollars in 100 dollar bills. Not a bad night's work, Bouchard thought.

On the platform were five boxes, each weighing 100 pounds. The boxes were swung over the side and onto *Andiamo*'s deck by a small portable crane. Bouchard noticed that the yacht's deck was covered with multiple layers of rubber blankets. Fragile stuff, he thought, but immediately reminded himself that it was none of his business.

⊶ ⊷

The transaction completed, Bouchard raised his cap in a friendly salute to Mr. Jones.

Three of Mr. Jones' crewmembers raised their silencer-equipped pistols and opened fire, killing Bouchard and his men. Twelve more swarmed aboard the freighter. They knew that there were 20 other crewmembers aboard, and they fanned out through the ship to hunt them down and kill them. Four *Andiamo* crewmembers then went to pre-selected locations along the hull of the freighter where they placed heavy bags of plastique explosives at spots below the water line. They set the timers and left the vessel. Eight other men ran through the ship to kill any straggling crewmembers and to open any watertight doors and hatches.

Mr. Jones knew, from the plan that was devised by a colleague in Dubai, that the ship would sink less than a half-hour after the charges blew up. As *Andiamo* was about a mile from *The Sea Bounder*, Mr. Jones heard four muffled thrumps as the explosives detonated below the water line.

Andiamo continued her journey to the mouth of New York Harbor.

CHAPTER FORTY NINE

"No, Trevor," said Carlini, "we're not having a good day. The one thing your amazing algorithm didn't count on was a decoy, or at least a plan to move the bombs to a different site. Your thoughts are most welcome."

"Na worry, mates." Trevor said. "Did you think your Aussie friend left his brains down undah?"

"Do you have some alternatives, some other sites, anything?" said Buster.

"Of course I do," said Trevor, as if we were all mathematically impaired. "Denver (*Denvah*) was the most logical bomb plant according to the algorithm, but I wrote the program to also spit up what I call anomalies, pieces that don't fit together, things that just don't look right. And here's my number one anomaly: an expensive yacht purchase. Now I know that you're thinking, what's the big deal with some Middle Eastern guy using his oil money to buy a luxury yacht. But the timing is interesting. Twenty Million bucks was transferred from a bank in Yemen to a bank in Fort Lauderdale, Florida, and then transferred from that bank to a yacht brokerage."

"Do you have a name for the bank account, Trevor?" asked Buster.

"No, Buster, I don't, but that should be an easy job for you guys. Hell, this isn't Switzerland."

Buster excused himself and left the room. He returned 10 minutes later.

"The account is with Bank of America and is in the name of a Gordon Jones. I've identified the yacht he bought. In a few minutes I'll have the name of the boat, assuming he renamed it. We're running a name check on Gordon Jones, but I doubt we'll find anything."

"Pardon me, gentlemen," said Carlini, "but I'm not sure I see a connection to what we're looking for."

"Mr. Director," said Buster, "Trevor's exactly right when he and his algorithm look for anomalies. And how's this for an anomaly? This Jones guy bought the yacht just last week, a 20 Million-dollar-yacht, and it's already left port. If you spent that kind of money on an expensive toy, wouldn't you leave it in dock for at least a few days or weeks to make sure everything is working?"

"But if it left port, how the hell do we know where it is?" asked Carlini.

"My satellite people are already on it," said Buster. "With the size, 85 feet, an estimated time of departure, and an estimated cruising speed, we should be able to ID the boat within an hour."

"Folks," said Carlini, "sitting around this conference table are some of the smartest people I've ever met in my life, and I'm not just blowing smoke. I think it's time to put our collective brain power to work. Let's start looking for some dots to connect."

"Mr. Director," said Bennie, "I'd like a recording of what you just said about smart people so I can email it to my mother."

We all laughed. Bennie, the friendly shrink, had eyeballed the need for some levity in the room.

"If I may," continued Ben, "I'll admit to being a bit stumped. We went from an old Chrysler plant in Detroit where the bombs were kept that were targeted for the ships. Then we found the Denver plant, thanks to

Trevor. It's pretty safe to assume, given Joe Monahan's description and Janice's drawing, that Denver was definitely a bomb plant. But then, to overstate the obvious, we came up empty. With the clock ticking, do we dare put all of our eggs in a basket that looks like a yacht? I'd like to hear Trevor's thoughts on this."

"You're right on target, Ben," said Trevor. "Never (*nevah*) put all your eggs in the same basket. Whoever came up with that quote should have a statue erected to him at Harvard Business School. So here's the other basket, or baskets, that we should look at. You folks have told me about the list of al Qaeda safe houses you got from that fella Joe Monahan. These haven't been plugged into my algorithm yet, but it seems logical that we should put surveillance on them as well."

"Already done," said Buster. "They're under 24/7 satellite surveillance."

Carlini laughed. "Buster," he said, "when this is all over I'd like to cut a business deal with you. I'm thinking of setting up a company that sells action figures named 'Buster.' You squeeze it and an electronic voice says, 'Done it already.'"

"Thanks for the compliment, sir," said Buster. "If it weren't for this job I think I'd just be an average obsessive compulsive lying on a couch and talking to somebody like Bennie. But getting back to Ben's question, I think we'd all like Trevor to give us his thoughts about the yacht."

With that, Buster's pager went off. He only accepts calls from Phil Lopez, his aide, and Phil knows to call only when it's an absolute necessity.

"Before Trevor gives us his yacht ideas I want to give you all an update. That was Phil Lopez. It seems the yacht is named *Andiamo*, but most importantly, it has just been tracked going up the Hudson River, near the George Washington Bridge. What we don't know is if the boat made any stops between Fort Lauderdale and its present location. But what we do know is that we've got it in our sights."

"Denver was a shock, to say the least," said Carlini. "But we're no longer back to square one."

CHAPTER FIFTY

It's 5:45 AM on October 29th. I'm in Frank's apartment again, having slept over after last night's seemingly endless meeting. I like it here. Frank likes having me here. And that's all I have to say about that.

I always wake up automatically at 5:30, so I was in the kitchen making coffee. At 8 AM we are due in the Director's office for, you guessed it, another meeting.

The phone rang. I assumed it was Buster. Who else would call at 5:45 AM?

Frank picked up the phone and walked into the kitchen yawning. We kissed and suddenly Frank appeared to snap to attention.

"Yes, sir," Frank said. Then he said it again. And again.

I'm dying to know who "sir" is. Admiral Frank is usually on the receiving end of "sir."

I stood with my face 4 inches from his, just to make sure he had privacy.

"It's the White House." Frank scribbled on a piece of paper.

I stared with a look that, I don't know, must have seemed dumbfounded, because I *was* dumfounded.

As I stared intently at Frank I poured him a cup of hot coffee. Shit, I forgot the cup! I poured the hot coffee on his left hand, which was resting on the counter.

Frank danced around in obvious pain, trying to keep his voice calm on the phone. I grabbed him by the arm and led him to the sink where I ran his hand under cold water. I walked to the other side of the kitchen and poured Frank another coffee, this time remembering the cup.

After Frank said "yes, sir," for the zillionth time, give or take, he finally hung up the phone, but not without a final "yes, sir."

"So who were you talking to?" I said, as I rubbed burn cream over the back of Frank's hand.

"The President himself."

"Holy shit!" I said, somehow thinking that was an appropriate thing to say.

"He wants me to take command of a Carrier Strike Group. It seems that the White House is worried that if we don't stop the Thanksgiving bombs, some hostile nations will want to take advantage of the situation."

"What exactly is a Carrier Strike Group?" I asked.

"It's a group of ships consisting of an aircraft carrier, a guided missile cruiser, and at least two frigates or large destroyers. It used to be called a Carrier Battle Group. My flagship, which is the carrier I'll be aboard, is none other than the *USS Abraham Lincoln*, my old friend Ashley Patterson's ship. The force will be known as Carrier Strike Group 1115, named after Thanksgiving of this year."

I almost reacted like a jerk, but I'm pleased that I got it together in time. My first thoughts were how dangerous will it be and when will I see Frank again. But then I quickly realized that Frank is an important man, important enough to get a call from the President of the United States himself. Frank's job is to defend our country. My job is to help him do just that.

I can start by not pouring coffee on his hand.

CHAPTER FIFTY ONE

B ennie Weinberg here.

I walked down the long corridor leading to Buster's office. I think Buster planned his office to be located at the end of a long hallway to give visitors time to assemble their thoughts before meeting with him.

A short, attractive redhead walked toward me, coming from Buster's office. She was quite shapely and wore an expensive, tasteful dark gray business suit, which complimented her mane of red hair. The closer we got the more familiar she looked.

"Bennie," she yelled. Obviously I must know her. Time to think fast and remember faster.

"Maggie, Maggie Cohen!" I yelled back.

We hugged as only old friends do. She wore perfume that I remember well. My studies tell me that the olfactory sense is a key repository of recollection, and the scent of her brought back some wonderful memories of times past. Maggie and I met at Harvard when I was in the medical school and she was studying for a PhD in political science.

After we hugged we continued to hold each other. My shy introverted personality was starting to reassert itself. Yes, loudmouth, trash-talking Bennie Weinberg is a closet introvert, something that people find surprising. I know, as a psychiatrist, that resisting an emotion will not make it go away, so I just allowed myself to feel shy. Shy but excited at the same time.

Maggie was a dead ringer for Bette Midler, only a bit more shapely if you can believe it.

My phone buzzed. It was Buster.

"Bennie," said Buster, "I'm sorry but we have to delay our meeting for an hour. I'll see you later."

It was the best message I ever got from Buster. I had an hour to spare, and somebody to share it with.

"You look like you could use a cup of coffee," I said, trying to sound charming but somehow feeling that I didn't achieve the result. "We can catch up on old times."

"You're on, Handsome," Maggie said. "How about my favorite cafeteria?"

Handsome? Not to brag, but I'm the nation's top expert in judging a person's veracity. Nobody bullshits Bennie Weinberg. Maggie was telling the truth, not that I'm objectively handsome, but she *believed* what she said. I hoped it wasn't obvious but I felt myself blushing.

We found a quiet corner of the CIA cafeteria and sipped our coffee, our hands touching all the while. I figured it was time to get the normal "long time no see" pleasantries out of the way, so I gave Maggie a brief recent history of Bennie Weinberg for the past 20 years.

I reviewed my life since Harvard, including my divorce, a part of my background that still bothers me. To dispel any confusion, I also discussed my friendship with Jack Thurber and my time travelling experiences, which brought me to the CIA. I then talked about how great she looked, how 20 years actually made her look better. Just as I don't accept bullshit from people, I don't indulge in it myself. I meant it. Maggie looked gorgeous, better than ever. Her perfume anchored my olfactory senses to a time in the past, a happy time. The only thing that ever came between Maggie and me were circumstances. After she finished her PhD she went to Oxford University as a visiting scholar. I met the lady who would become my first wife, and Maggie met some guy from Oxford, married him and divorced a year later. We gradually lost touch. Sometimes you wonder why that happens, but it does, and it did.

Maggie is now a professor of political science at Georgetown, specializing in the Middle East. Like me, she's been deputized as a provisional CIA agent. She's completely up to speed on the upcoming Thanksgiving crisis and is on paid leave from Georgetown to work full time at the Agency, most often with Buster.

"Bennie, you look great," said Maggie as she squeezed my hand. She still seems to be telling the truth. Maybe she has astigmatism. I'm glad that I've taken Jack Thurber's advice that I lose weight and work out every day. I've lost seven pounds in the last three weeks. But I haven't grown back any of my missing hair.

Maggie reached over an patted my bald top.

"I love it," she said. "It looks sexy."

I still don't detect any bullshit, but so what? If she's lying, I'm liking it, true or not.

We kept on sharing information about ourselves as if we were cramming for an exam. Over the years Maggie had become quite a scholar on the Middle East, hence the interest of the CIA. I tiptoed into the subject area of other men. There are none, which I had a hard time believing, but again, I didn't detect any lies.

The hour was drawing to a close and I dare not be late for a meeting with Buster.

"I'd like to ask you out on a date," I said, trying to conjure up my inner romantic.

"I'd love that," said Maggie, "but we're all on lockdown until this crisis is over."

"When can I see you again," I asked.

"How about all the time," Maggie said, squeezing my hand.

In the past month I've gone through enough weirdness for an average lifetime. Shuttling back and forth through a wormhole and working to prevent a nuclear disaster has consumed my time, to say the least. But this morning is the most amazing event I've experienced since I can remember. I met an old girl friend who's brilliant, beautiful, and single.

And she thinks my bald head is sexy.

CHAPTER FIFTY TWO

I walked into Buster's office right on time, which is the way Buster demands. I guess my meeting with Maggie still showed on my face.

"What's the goofy grin all about, Bennie?" asked Buster.

"It's about one of your researchers, Maggie Cohen, an old and maybe a new girlfriend," I said. "Long story. Do you mind if I continue to grin?"

Buster raised his eyebrows as if to say, "yes I'd like to hear about it, but not now."

We walked into the conference room.

Sitting around the table were Janice, Admiral Frank, and none other than Joe Monahan, legs shackled to the floor. I noticed that Frank's left hand was bandaged.

"We're going to lose Admiral Frank," said Buster, "who's just been given command of a Carrier Strike Group, so I wanted him to be here for some last minute brain-storming. Congratulations, Admiral. Our loss but the country's gain."

"I've invited (how do you invite a prisoner?) Joe Monahan so we can review the shocker that we got last night," Buster continued. "Joe, here's the bottom line. The drawing that you and Janice made from your memory of the bomb plant, plus the brilliant sleuth work of Trevor McMartin, pointed us at a building in Denver. With the help of Janice we tunneled under the building, intending to soak it in tear gas. What we found was nothing except for five empty suitcases. But Trevor may have come up with a new target. Now I'm going to ask you a few questions. First, does the name Woody Bouchard mean anything to you?"

"Bouchard, yes," said Joe Monahan, "but Woody doesn't ring a bell. I seem to recall the word 'captain' in front of Bouchard."

"How about Jones, Gordon Jones?" said Buster.

"Never heard of him."

"Joe," said Buster, "as you're aware, you don't have *jack shit* for a security clearance, but the clock is ticking so I'm going to let you in on some Top Secret information. Trevor isolated an 85-foot yacht that may be involved in the plot. By dumb luck, we have a satellite photo of a freighter captained by a Woody Bouchard off the coast of Long Island next to a yacht. We weren't even looking for it at the time, but came across the satellite photo. Other photos show that the freighter exploded and sank after the yacht pulled away. We picked up the image of the yacht just south of the George Washington Bridge on the Hudson River. The boat was purchased by a man named Gordon Jones with money wired from Yemen. The name of the yacht is *Andiamo*."

Joe Monahan rubbed his face and held up his hand to ask for silence while he scribbled some notes.

"The name *Sea Bounder* comes to my mind. I remember the name coming up in the same discussions as Bouchard. Those conversations also included the name *Andiamo*. I wasn't directly involved in any of the discussions, I just overheard them. Remember, al Qaeda has become fanatical about limiting information only to those with an absolute need to know. But all that is beside the point. If your theory is correct, that this yacht is transporting the bombs, we may have a gigantic problem. Three words that you said, Buster, are the scariest I've heard in this meeting: George Washington Bridge. If your premise is accurate, and if this wormhole business is in any way true, we know that the future will involve the destruction of lower Manhattan. If you caught *Andiamo* at the George Washington Bridge, that means they already dropped off at least one bomb. I doubt that they're looking to blow up Tarrytown. One nuke has already been planted, somewhere south of the George Washington Bridge."

"Joe," said Admiral Frank, "we need you to plumb the depths of your excellent memory. We need you to come up with some dots. Don't worry about connecting them."

"Admiral," said Joe, "whatever talents I may have, speaking and understanding Arabic isn't one of them. I was able to pick up words here and there, but I can't recall the syntax or relevance. Maybe Doctor Ben over here can help."

⟞⟞ ⟝⟝

"I *can* help," I said. "Hypnosis is one of the tools in my bag of tricks. Under hypnosis your subconscious mind comes up with stuff that your conscious mind blocks. Thoughts will appear that never registered in your consciousness before. So let me ask you a question, are you willing to undergo hypnosis? Hypnotic suggestion works best when the subject is willing. So how about it, Joe?"

"I think I've made it clear from our previous meetings, I don't care if you people water board me. I want to stop the bombs. Please, Doctor Ben, do what you have to do."

"Buster," I said, "I know you like to practice music on the piano upstairs. Do you have a metronome?"

Buster bolted from the conference room into his office and returned with a metronome, a perfect device for inducing a hypnotic trance.

"Now, Joe," I said, "I'm going to ask you to focus on the arm of the metronome as it tick tocks back and forth. Tick tock, tick tock, tick tock. You're feeling relaxed, even drowsy. Tick tock, tick tock, tick tock. Your left arm wants to point toward the ceiling. Now it wants to return to the table. Joe, I'm going to suggest a list of words and tell me whatever comes into your mind."

"World Trade Center."

"9/11"

"Statue of Liberty."

"Class trip in grammar school."

"City Hall."

"Mayor of the City."

"Wall Street."

"Location?"

"I say again, Wall Street."

"Van."

"Wall Street."

"Bomb."

"Wall Street."

"Explosion."

"Does the bomb explode on Wall Street?"

"Yes."

"Where on Wall Street?"

"Location?"

"Trinity Church?"

"Location?"

"New York Stock Exchange?"

"Explosion."

"Color of the van?"

"Burgundy."

"Markings on the van?"

"White lettering."

"What did the lettering say?"

"Ajax Plumbing Supply."

I turned off the metronome, snapped my fingers and patted Joe on the arm. He shook his head, yawned, and looked around the room.

"Your subconscious thoughts, Joe, seem to indicate that one of the bombs will be placed in a van in front of the New York Stock Exchange. Does that bring any recollection to mind?"

Joe closed his eyes and said nothing for a full minute.

"Nothing, Doctor Ben. I have no recollection of that at all."

I slipped back into bullshit detector mode. "The guy's telling the truth," I announced.

Janice raised her hand, not wanting to blurt out anything that would come between Joe and me.

"Bennie," said Janice, "is it possible that these subconscious recollections come from a dream or a nightmare?"

"Good question, Janice," I said. "The answer is 'yes,' The subconscious gets its data from a number of sources. But what we have here is a hint, a clue, a dot to connect. Hypnosis isn't an exact science, but it's a tool."

Buster dialed his cellphone. Within a half-hour the Central Intelligence Agency knew more about Ajax Plumbing Supply than the rest of the world would care to ask.

It's either a dream or a way to prevent a nightmare.

CHAPTER FIFTY THREE

They that go down to the sea in ships, that do business in great waters; These see the works of the LORD, and his wonders in the deep. For He commandeth, and raiseth the stormy wind, which lifteth up the waves thereof. They mount up to the heavens, they go down again to the depths: their soul is melted because of trouble. They reel to and fro, and stagger like a drunken man, and are at their wits' end. Then they cry unto the LORD in their trouble, and He bringeth them out of their distresses. He maketh the storm a calm, so that the waves thereof are still. Then are they glad because they be quiet; so He bringeth them unto their desired haven.
Psalm 107:23-30, King James Version

➤+ +➤

War has come between lovers since the dawn of history, and it was about to happen to Frank and me. Our brief time together was a lot more than a whirlwind romance. It's a lot deeper than that. We'd known each other for about three weeks but it felt like we'd been together for a lifetime. I know that sounds sudsy, but I think part of it has to do with time travel and the bizarre crisis that we faced. It's like our souls melded. Corny I know, dramatic I'm sure, but it's the friggin' truth. Frankie and I love each other.

Frank was due to report aboard the *USS Abraham Lincoln* the next morning and take command of Carrier Strike Group 1115, named in honor of Thanksgiving 2015, less than a month away. Frank has gone over with me what he'll be up to, within the confines of security, of course. The impending nuclear attacks have caused the White House to take some radical actions, one of them being the creation of four Carrier Strike Groups that will sail close to the shores of the United States.

It's mainly a show of force, Frank assured me, a way of flexing our muscles in front of the world, reminiscent of our original flag, a rattle snake coiled near the words "Don't Tread on Me." With the firepower and technology that Frank will command, a new flag would appropriately say, "Don't even *think* about treading on me."

Frank said that he doesn't expect to see danger or even much action. Even if the nuclear Thanksgiving attacks came to happen, and that's what the White House is worried about, it's unlikely that a foreign hostile power would dare to attack us. But it's a big *IF*. With five American cities devastated by nuclear bombs, the nation would be a lot weaker. Our Navy would become our main line of defense.

"How's your hand, Frank?" I inquired, asking about the damage I inflicted by pouring coffee without a cup.

"It's feeling much better, Hon. At least it didn't burn my fingers so I can still pinch your cute little ass." With that, he did.

"I'm feeling a lot better about the latest intelligence since our last meeting in Buster's office," I said. "It looks like we've narrowed the bomb locations and this crap may soon be over. But who knows. The last three weeks have been nothing but surprises, beginning with my picking up a handsome hitchhiker named Frank on the other side of a wormhole."

"I share your guarded optimism, Honey. The next few days and weeks are going to be rough, but I think we're closing in on a solution. We've got great people working on the crisis, not to mention the beautiful lady in front of me. Add Buster to the mix and I wouldn't want to be on the other side. He solves problems before other people even see them."

"Now I want you to make me a promise," Frank continued. "A lot of unexpected stuff is going to roll down the hill in the next few weeks. You're a tough lady, and that's one of the things I love about you. But remember this, please. Our mission, yours and mine, has nothing to do with anger or hatred or fear. I know I've spoken to you about this before, but I want to remind you. Just think about the mission and how to get it done. Negative emotions have no place in this strange time. Watch Buster. He's the most mission focused guy I've ever met. So that's what I want you to promise me. You will focus on the mission, the task at hand, whatever it may be at the time."

"Yes, I promise," I said. "When a man like you gives me advice, I think I'd be pretty stupid not to listen."

"But I have something I'd like you to focus on, Frankie."

"What is it, Hon?"

"Let's make love. Mad hot love."

CHAPTER FIFTY FOUR

The shrill sound of the bosun's pipe sounded throughout the *USS Abraham Lincoln.*

"Carrier Strike Group 1115 Arriving." This is the Navy's traditional way of announcing the arrival of a dignitary, along with that person's official position. Admiral Frank Thompson, commanding officer of Carrier Strike Group 1115, bounded up the gangplank, saluted the flag at the stern of the ship, and then saluted the Officer of the Deck on duty on the quarterdeck.

"Welcome aboard, Admiral," said Lieutenant Figueroa, the Officer of the Deck. "Sergeant Jenkins will show you to your quarters, Sir."

Marine Sergeant Jenkins, assisted by a corporal, picked up the admiral's bags and the three headed for Frank's new home, known as Flag Country on the *USS Abraham Lincoln.* His quarters were comfortable and his office was large, unnecessarily large thought Frank. Defense contractors know who to impress, and a lot of taxpayer dollars are spent on the brass who make the procurement decisions.

While the captain and her crew manned the ship's bridge, Frank's at-sea station was the flag bridge, one level below.

Admiral Frank's aide was Commander Ezekiel (Zeke) Jefferson. Zeke was a 6'4" black man. He played tight end at the Naval Academy. Zeke was well known among his friends as an outgoing "people person," a guy who would light up a room with his humor and friendliness. But his face always appeared to wear a scowl, a feature that suited Zeke just fine. As an officer on his way up in his career, he found it convenient to be able to intimidate people with his face, beneath which lurked a smile. His job as admiral's aide was important, and Zeke's gruff appearance helped to get things done.

The date was October 30, less than a month to Thanksgiving Day. The *Lincoln* was scheduled to put to sea the next morning, October 31, 2015.

Frank spent the day meeting with various department heads and conferring by secure phone with the Office of Naval Operations. At 6:30 PM (1830) he sat down to coffee with his friend Ashley Patterson, the Commanding Officer of the *USS Abraham Lincoln*, after they had supper together.

"I don't expect trouble, Ashley, but of course you and I know that our job *is* to expect trouble. I've gone down your checklist and everything looks like it's a go. We sail at 0700 tomorrow. So tell me, my friend, how is everything with you? We haven't had much of a chance to talk in the last few days."

"Frank, I've just gone through the weirdest time of my life, and I'm including my four months in the year 1861 in that *Gray Ship* incident."

"Weirder than *The Gray Ship*?" said Frank. "Now that *is* weird."

"Well, listen to this and tell me if it isn't weird. Three months ago my time travelling husband disappeared, then came back and said that if we don't act fast the *Lincoln* and four other ships will get nuked, killing 26,000 people including Jack and me. So we stopped those attacks and then you came through the wormhole with Janice and blew the whistle on Plan B, the attacks that are supposed to happen less than a month from now. If so much life wasn't on the line I'd almost laugh. But to change the subject, my time travelling friend, how's everything with you? I hear that you and Janice have become an item."

"Yes, Ashley, we have become an item, more than an item. I feel like a kid who's just fallen in love. When this chaos is over things will become more serious with me and Janice, long term serious."

"You know I was jealous of Janice when I first met her. From snippets of conversations I heard from Ben and Wally I suspected that she was after Jack, big time. He was gone for three weeks in 2017 time and three months in 2015. I can see how he may have been tempted by such an attractive woman, especially not knowing if I was still alive."

"Ashley, you've just given me an opening to tell you some things about your husband that you may not know. Janice and I have pretty much shared our lives over the last few weeks. There are no secrets between us. Now I'm going to share some things with you. When Jack showed up in 2017 claiming that he came from the past, from 2015, Janice thought he was a bit nuts. She was convinced, given the history that people knew in 2017, that you were dead, killed in the attack on the *Lincoln*. She thought that Jack somehow missed the sailing that day and managed to survive. Ashley, Janice was convinced that Jack was a handsome widower. According to Janice, Jack never stopped loving you or talking about you. She admitted to me that she flirted with Jack non-stop, but when she eventually learned that the past could be changed and that Jack could save your life and his, she backed off. Janice thinks the world of you, and Jack. She thinks of Jack as a friend."

"Frank, I love Jack and trust him, but hearing what you just said from a good friend like you means the world to me. Thank you."

"Captain, you've got an aircraft carrier to drive tomorrow, and I know you have a lot to do. You should hit the rack early tonight."

"Good night, and thanks again, Frank."

"I'm glad I could clear up any lingering doubt, Ashley. Good night."

CHAPTER FIFTY FIVE

Buster requested a quick meeting with Director Carlini. He brought Janice and Bennie with him in the unlikely event he forgot something.

"The subject of this meeting," said Buster, "is Ajax Plumbing Supply. It's a name that Joe Monahan recalled from the hypnotic state that Dr. Ben put him in. As I briefed you earlier, Sir, that same hypnosis session narrowed the possible bomb location to Wall Street, specifically the New York Stock Exchange. Monahan remembered a van, that it was colored burgundy, and it bore the imprint Ajax Plumbing Supply."

"Buster, at your earlier briefing you discussed hypnosis. I'm familiar with it as a method of interrogation, but I'm also aware that it has limitations. How do we know that this Ajax company isn't just a figment of his dreams?"

"I've chased down Ajax Plumbing Supply, Mr. Director, and found some interesting stuff. The company was incorporated in New York just a month ago. I've interviewed a couple of people in the plumbing supply business, and they told me that these outfits usually have a whole fleet of vans and trucks because, as a supply company, they have to deliver products all over the city. Ajax Plumbing Supply has only one vehicle, a burgundy van. I've put out an all-points bulletin through the NYPD and the New York office of the FBI. Nothing's turned up yet. A further check of Ajax Plumbing Supply shows that its beginning bank account balance was $15,000, nothing to be amazed at, but the source of the funding is interesting. Our friend Trevor traced the money to the Middle East. There was a wire transfer to the company's bank account from Saudi Arabia on the day it became incorporated. The corporate records don't show much, just a local lawyer as the 'sole incorporator,' a common way of starting a new corporation. But the attorney's name is Ali Houmed. He's been on the FBI watch list for over three years ever since he was implicated as a possible accomplice in the Shoe Bomber case. These are big dots, Mr. Director. A plumbing supply company with one van, no advertising, and a lawyer on a watch list. The only thing that can slow down our all points search is if the van is parked in a garage somewhere."

"Does Ajax Plumbing Supply have a telephone number?" Asked Carlini. "Why not just call them and ask for a delivery of some plumbing supplies?"

"No phone number, Sir. It seems like this is a company that doesn't want to do any business."

"Hold on," said Janice. "Why doesn't somebody call the attorney, Ali Houmed, and say they saw the name on recent incorporations list and ask if they'd be interested in some special plumbing supply software. I have a nephew who works in sales with a software outfit. They prospect for new business all the time by looking up new incorporations and finding the names of companies that could use their programs. Because Ajax has the simple description, Plumbing Supply, nobody would smell anything weird about a phone call like that."

"But what happens when attorney Houmed says, 'my client's not interested?'" said Bennie.

"Good point, Ben," said Carlini. "I'm sure that's exactly what he'd say. These people have nothing to do with plumbing supplies, so why should he be interested in specialized software."

"No, I hate to say this but the only way we're going to locate that van is through old fashioned police work. When, I don't want to say *if*, some cop locates the van we need him to place a GPS tracker on it. Buster, you need to have your guys work the phones and stress with every law enforcement official how important this search is. I think we should put our concentration on lower Manhattan, because the yacht presumably dropped off one of the bombs there. Also, make sure you apply for a warrant from the Foreign Intelligence Surveillance Court so we can plant the tracker legally."

"That's already been done, Mr. Director."

"Why does that not surprise me, Buster?"

"Okay, folks, our field seems to have narrowed. We have satellite and drone surveillance of the yacht *Andiamo*. From Buster's research it appears that Ajax Plumbing Supply is not a figment of Joe Monahan's imagination. So that leaves four bombs in the yacht, plus one intended for Wall Street."

"Today's October 31st. Thanksgiving is getting closer."

CHAPTER FIFTY SIX

"Captain," said the Officer of the Deck, we have a foreign warship steaming about two miles off our starboard beam. It appears to be an Iranian Alvand Class frigate. She's accompanied by two Bayandor Class patrol frigates."

"Any sign of hostile intent, Lieutenant?"

"Well, Ma'am, two miles off our beam puts them well within the 12-mile territorial limit of U.S. waters."

"Signal bridge, this is the captain. Send a message to that warship off our starboard beam to withdraw to a location beyond United States territorial limits immediately."

Ashley then called the Admiral's bridge.

"Admiral, this is the Captain. I'm calling to advise you that three Iranian frigates are a couple of miles off our starboard beam and are within U.S. territorial limits. You're welcome to join me on the bridge, Sir."

Admiral Thompson was on the bridge within a minute.

"This is amazingly brazen, Fran..., I mean Admiral. To invade our limits and to head straight for a Carrier Strike Force seems insane. I'm prepared to attack if they get any closer."

"I concur, Captain. Launch at your discretion." said Admiral Thompson.

"Lieutenant, sound general quarters," Ashley said to the OOD.

A loud clanging, ear shattering alarm went off throughout the ship, followed by the announcement:

GENERAL QUARTERS, GENERAL QUARTERS, ALL HANDS MAN YOUR BATTLE STATIONS. THIS IS NOT A DRILL. REPEAT, THIS IS NOT A DRILL.

Ashley called the flight officer to alert him to maneuver six F/A-18E Super Hornet fighter jets on deck and ready them for a launch.

During the standoff, while they awaited the Iranian reply, Ashley leaned over to Admiral Thompson while she put on her helmet and said, "You know Frank, I'd love to be on the flight deck in one of those Hornets."

"You stay put, Ashley," said Admiral Frank. "I haven't driven one of these things in years. I need you here on the bridge."

"Signal bridge, this is the Captain. Repeat the message to our inquisitive neighbor."

"Aye aye, Captain."

"INCOMING, STARBOARD BEAM" screamed the OOD at the top of his voice as a missile shrieked toward the *Lincoln*. The *Lincoln* automatically launched 12 anti-missile rockets.

Everyone on the bridge was gripped by a few seconds of abject horror. You only get one chance to stop an anti-ship missile headed your way. Fortunately the *Lincoln*'s rockets did their job and the missile exploded a few hundred yards away.

"Launch aircraft," Ashley said to the flight deck officer. "Attack and destroy the frigates."

As the first Hornet cleared the flight deck with a roar, the OOD again yelled "INCOMING, STARBOARD BEAM!"

The missile screamed toward the *Lincoln* as yet another battery of anti-missile rockets deployed. This time the *Lincoln* wasn't so lucky. The missile was only about 100 yards from the ship when it was exploded by a rocket, but not soon enough to prevent a cloud of shrapnel from hurtling toward the ship. Ashley watched an array of antennas topple toward the flight deck, some of it landing on a plane.

The Hornets raced toward their targets. On command from Admiral Thompson, all three of the *Lincoln's* support ships fired Harpoon anti-ship missiles at the Iranian frigates. All three Iranian ships were destroyed and sank in less than five minutes.

Ashley and Frank looked at each other.

"These fucking Iranians are out of their minds," Ashley said to Frank in a tone only he could hear.

"I'm going to the flag bridge," said Frank. "I'll order our support ships to keep on station except for one frigate that I'll assign to look for survivors."

"Aye aye, Sir." said Ashley.

"Shall I secure from general quarters, Captain?" asked the OOD.

"No, not until I order it. I don't want people breaking their necks over debris. As soon as the battle damage assessment team lets me know we're okay, I'll give you the word."

"Aye aye, Captain."

———

In 15 minutes Ashley ordered the OOD to secure from general quarters, enabling the crew to leave their battle stations.

"Captain, this is Admiral Thompson. I just spoke to the Office of Naval Operations. They want the *Lincoln* to pull back into Norfolk for battle repair. We should be there for three or four days. NavOps has alerted the White House and the State Department."

"Commander," Ashley said to the ship's navigator, "set course for Norfolk."

Admiral Frank returned to the bridge and walked over to Captain Ashley, who was sitting in the Captain's chair.

"I neglected to say something during all the excitement, Ashley."

"What is it Frank?"

"Seldom have I seen such a display of combat effectiveness. Job well done. I'm putting you in for a commendation. Pretty soon you and I can pal around as a couple of fellow admirals."

"Thanks Frank, I really appreciate that, especially coming from you. You know, this is the first time I've been in combat since the Civil War in 1861. Back then all we had to worry about were cannon balls."

Thompson laughed. Time travelers always have strange stories to tell each other.

CHAPTER FIFTY SEVEN

J anice here.

I must admit that I totally freaked out when I heard that the *Lincoln* had been attacked. It's been all over the news this morning. Frankie, God bless him, called me at 8 AM as soon as he could get cellphone reception. Apparently a lot of the ship's communication antennas were knocked out during the attack. The ship has tied up at the dock in Norfolk for a few days of repairs.

Just hearing his voice calmed me down. I asked him how his burned hand was doing. Sometimes I come up with the lamest things to say when I'm nervous. We exchanged "I love you," something I'll never get tired of. Frank, who obviously had a busy day in front of him, promised to call me again later in the day at 1730. That's 5:30 PM to you and me.

I was busy with Buster projects, something he never seemed to run out of.

5:30 PM rolled around and the phone didn't ring. I was sure Frank was in a meeting or something. No big deal. Bennie and his pretty new friend Maggie asked me to have dinner with them, but I demurred. I was too nervous for socializing.

My stomach was now in a knot. 6:30 PM came and went and I was starting to feel nauseous. I know, I'll call Ashley. What will I say? "Have you seen a handsome admiral running around looking for a phone?"

I hesitated to call Ashley, feeling embarrassed. I busied myself with a Buster project. But now it was 7:15.

Fuck it, I'm calling Ashley.

Ashley picked up the phone on the first ring.

"Janice, hi." Ashley said in a soft voice.

"Ashley, I'm so sorry to bother you. God knows how busy you must be. Not everybody goes through a sea battle without details to sort out." I thought I was being quite pleasant and conversational.

"Ashley, where's Frank?" I finally blurted, a bit loudly.

"Oh, Janice, Honey, I was going to call you."

Ashley Patterson is one tough cookie. She speaks in what military types call a command voice. When Ashley opens her mouth, missiles fire, planes launch, people snap to attention. But that wasn't the Ashley Patterson I heard on the phone. I didn't hear the command voice of a military leader. I heard a big sister, speaking softly and trying to console me, trying to say "everything will be alright."

"I just got off the phone with Buster, Janice."

Ashley paused to take a breath, a long pause, a seemingly endless pause.

"Janice, we don't know where Frank is."

If I had a choice between a 10-kiloton nuke and what I just heard, I think I'd go for the bomb.

I knew my next question would sound obvious, but I asked it anyway.

"What do you mean he's missing? Where is he? How can he be missing?"

"Janice, here's what we know. First, he didn't fall overboard. I personally saw him after we tied up. Also, I ordered a search of the entire ship, as is required in a circumstance like this. I had a detail team go over every square inch of the *Lincoln*. All we know at this point is that Frank is not aboard. I've tried his cellphone just as you have. Nothing, as you know. The White House and Director Carlini have been notified. About the most positive thing I can tell you at this point is that Buster is on the case. I'll call you when I hear anything, and I ask you to do the same. I know that you and Frank are in love. I know that because he told me. Frank is also a good friend of mine. Janice, we'll find him."

After I got off the phone with Ashley I called Buster. His phone was busy. I took off my shoes and sprinted barefoot to his office with my heels under my arm. I opened the door without knocking. Buster was still on the phone, but he looked as if he expected me and motioned me in. He hung up the phone.

"Buster, do we have any idea where he is?" I thought the question was dumb, just a space filler to mask my emotions. I was amazed at Buster's answer.

"We know exactly where he is."

CHAPTER FIFTY EIGHT

F rank Thompson was lashed to a chair with yards of rope. He could barely see through his almost closed eyelids, swollen from repeated punches to his face. He found it difficult to talk, his jaw having been fractured by a baseball bat.

Sheik Abbas Haddad stood in front of Thompson, holding a hunting knife.

"You heathen scum. You have betrayed your brothers and Islam itself. You will soon go to hell where you will rot for eternity, but first you will give me the information I require. What does the CIA know about the bombs?"

"Nothing," Thompson mumbled as he winced in pain from the movement of his jaw. "They know nothing because I know nothing. You have kept this operation totally secret from everyone."

"What about the apostate Joseph Monahan? What did he tell them?"

"Monahan is dead," said Thompson. "He was killed in prison."

Another punch connected with Thompson's nose, delivered personally by Haddad.

"Your lies will only make it more painful for you," said Haddad.

CHAPTER FIFTY NINE

"Buster," I said. "How can you know where Frank is? I just spoke to Ashley Patterson. She has no idea."

"Janice, that's because Captain Patterson doesn't have a need to know. You should understand that by now."

"So where the hell is he and how do *you* know, and please don't give me any bullshit about my *need to know*."

"Frank is at an al Qaeda safe house, one of the places we identified from Joe Monahan's notes. It's about a half-hour from here. We know that because, with Frank's permission, we inserted a subcutaneous tracking device behind his right ear. We have his exact location."

"So now what?" I said. I'm sure I spoke too loudly but I couldn't help it.

"We have a hostage negotiating team ready to go. We're leaving right now. You stay here. I know this is rough on you, but you need to hang in there, Janice."

Buster headed for the door of his office.

I ran across the room and stood in front of him, blocking him from opening the door.

"Buster," I yelled in a way that was totally insubordinate but I didn't care." I'm coming with you."

"Janice, this is a sensitive mission. It requires experience. Also, things may get rough. You can't help us."

"Buster," I said in a lower and deeper tone as I looked into his eyes, "Name me one person, just one, in the entire Central Intelligence Agency, including yourself, who's a better shot than me."

Buster has a way of understanding things quickly, a way of sorting through all the background noise and seeing what's important. He pursed his lips and his shoulders sagged a bit, as if he knew he was about to concede a point.

"You come with me in the van."

CHAPTER SIXTY

CIA Director Carlini and Ben Weinberg entered Room 0116 to meet with Joe Monahan. Buster would normally be at a meeting like this but he was headed toward the safe house with the interrogation team.

"Joe," said Carlini, "we suddenly have an urgent situation and we need your help. Admiral Frank has been kidnapped by al Qaeda. We know his location, one of the safe houses you helped us ID, about a half-hour from here."

"When did they get him?" Monahan asked.

"As best we can figure about two hours ago. That's the last time anybody saw him on the *Lincoln*."

"Christ," said Joe, "about now he's wishing that he was dead."

Carlini winced at the thought.

"Joe, I know I'm fishing here, but is there anything you can tell us that may help?"

"You said you know exactly where he is, which tells me you've planted a tracking device on him."

"Well, Joe, you know I can't confirm that. Let's just say we know exactly where he is."

"Okay, I know, security clearance and all that. But let me ask you something. Assuming he's had a tracking device planted, which is obvious whether you confirm it or not, are you able to communicate with him? In other words, is there a subcutaneous microphone attached to the tracker?"

"Well, Joe, let's assume that we can, for the sake of argument. What are you thinking?"

"Tell him to give me up. I doubt that they believe the newspaper reports about my death. At this moment they're torturing Frank for information about me. Exchange me for Frank. In the scheme of things Mr. Director, wouldn't you trade a treasonous scumbag for a Navy Admiral?"

"I'm not sure I agree with the way you characterize yourself, Joe. At one time you were on a path to treason. You've now turned and redeemed yourself. I'm sitting here looking at a patriotic American. But that's beside the point. I don't see how this can work. They'd just kill you *and* Frank."

"If I may, Mr. Director," said Bennie. "I've been on more hostage negotiations than I can remember. Whenever there's a prisoner swap, things calm down, if only for a short time. It may work."

"Look at it this way," said Monahan. "I'm sure you have some of the best sharp shooters available on site. If Janice is there and armed, I almost pity the al Qaeda people. As soon as the exchange is made, your people come out blasting. If you're worried about me, and I'm not, you can give me body armor to improve my odds."

CHAPTER SIXTY ONE

"Here, put these on," said Buster, handing me a Kevlar vest and a helmet.

He then looked down at my bare feet and at the high heels I clutched under my arm. He rummaged through a chest and came out with a pair of high top Converse basketball sneakers and a package of three pairs of new sweat socks. The sneakers were about twice my size.

"These are mine," said Buster. "Wear extra sweat socks and it will help the fit."

I slipped the sneakers on, which was easy because they were so large. I was glad I chose to wear khaki slacks that morning rather than a skirt.

"How do I look?"

"Ridiculous, but so what?"

"Janice," you're one of the best people I've ever worked with, so don't take offense at what I'm about to tell you. I want you to follow my orders precisely. Don't wing it. This is a dangerous operation. We all have the same objective, to save Frank's life."

"Buster," I said. "I've learned to follow your leadership. Don't worry about me. Oh, I think I see a Sig P210 pistol hanging on the rack behind your head. It's not a cannon but it's about the most accurate handgun on the market. Would you be a love and hand it to me please."

Buster handed me the Sig.

"Thank you," I said, "now please give me that barrel extender." I connected the extender to the barrel of the Sig and pointed it to a corner to test the aim. A barrel extender increases the accuracy of the already accurate Sig.

"Want a couple of extra clips?" asked Buster.

"Just one," I said. "If I fire this thing it will be for accuracy. I don't expect to squeeze off more than two or three rounds. But I could use some extra clips for my Glock. Oh, and a couple of those concussion grenades please."

"Janice, please. You haven't been checked out on hand grenades. Stick with the guns."

"Buster, let me show you something. Please put one of the grenades in my hand."

He did.

"Here's the safety," I said, pointing, "and here's the triggering lever. So I remove the safety, activate the lever and throw it at the bad guys. By the way, I have a very strong throwing arm. Now do I really need a fucking eight-hour seminar to use this thing?"

"How many do you want?"

"Four should do the trick, thank you."

"How does your Kevlar vest feel, Janice?"

"Quite comfy. How does my helmet look?"

"Lovely. Janice, I'm not sure if you amaze me or scare me. You seem so calm."

"I've been coached by none other than Admiral Frank Thompson. Frankie, I mean Admiral Thomson, has drilled into my head the importance of the mission. No anger, no hatred, no fear. Just keep your eye on the goal, your focus on the mission. So yes, I'm calm. I'm on a mission, and you're the mission boss. Not really complicated, is it?"

"Janice, it's obvious to me over the past few days that you and Frank have become close. I think that's great, if you don't mind my opinion. I can't think of two finer people to be together. I'm just concerned that your affection for Frank may cloud your judgment. When we find him he may be in bad shape. Can you handle that?"

"Buster," I said, "we're on a mission. Simple as that."

CHAPTER SIXTY TWO

NYPD officer Phil Gribaldi, on routine foot patrol, walked down Bleecker Street in the Greenwich Village section of lower Manhattan. He came upon an alleyway to his right and peered down the distance as he was trained to do. Gribaldi knew that he wasn't paying attention to what he was doing. His wife had told him that morning that her sister and her husband would be coming up from Maryland to spend the weekend with them. He couldn't stand either of them and was wondering if he could find an excuse to vacate the house. Maybe he could trade overtime with one of the guys at the precinct. Gribaldi was ten feet beyond the alleyway when he stopped, an image having just clicked in his head. He walked back and stared at a burgundy colored van parked about 50 feet from the entrance to the alley. His precinct captain had put out the word to all personnel to be on the lookout for a burgundy van. He walked slowly toward the van, trying to avoid calling attention to himself. When he came alongside the vehicle he saw the inscription "Ajax Plumbing Supply." With visions of a commendation in his record, he bent down and faked tying his shoe as he placed a magnetic tracking device under the van's chassis. He stood up and clicked a few photos of the van from his Smartphone. He was also took photos of the walls of the building on each side of the van.

When he was a block from the alleyway he called Ike Washington, his precinct captain, having just emailed him the photos. Washington, according to the instructions from police headquarters, immediately called the office of the Commissioner of the NYPD. The commissioner, in turn, called Paul Bellamy, head of the New York field office of the FBI's Joint Terrorism Task Force. Bellamy immediately called CIA Director Bill Carlini.

⟞⟝ ⟞⟝

"Mr. Director, Paul Bellamy here. If you're in the need of any plumbing supplies, I think we found just the company for you."

CHAPTER SIXTY THREE

The CIA van, with the inscription "Higby Electric Contractors" on the side of its dented and faded white panel, pulled into the driveway of a home down the block from the al Qaeda safe house. Buster's people had rented the place at an exorbitant price that morning, saying they were from Paramount Pictures and needed the house for a movie scene, on the condition that the occupants vacate immediately. The driver pulled it around back so the van couldn't be seen from the street. Two other vans, both with the Higby Electric magnetic signs on their sides, pulled in behind the first. Joe Monahan was in one of the vehicles with Ben Weinberg sitting next to him.

The occupants of the vans, 18 armed agents in all, assembled behind the rented house. Buster addressed the group.

"Okay, folks, we've been through this drill countless times. It's a hostage situation, and the hostage is Navy Admiral Frank Thompson. Our objective is to take him with us safely. There's an interesting twist that's just been announced to me by Director Carlini. We have a prisoner to trade. As soon as the swap is completed, select your targets and open fire on my command. As the only one here who speaks Arabic, I will be the lead negotiator. Any questions?"

The group fanned out around the house in preselected positions. One of the vans was heavily armored, and Buster rode it to the front of the safe house. He spoke into a microphone and his words were transmitted by a powerful speaker on the other side of the van. Movie scenes usually feature an actor with a megaphone. After years of losing hostage negotiators with megaphones, modern law enforcement demanded a safer means of communication.

Buster began with the standard hostage negotiation conversation starter.

"The house is surrounded," said Buster in Arabic. "Lay down your arms and exit the building with your hands up and nobody will get hurt."

Silence. Buster repeated his demand.

A console operator in the van whispered to Buster that the tracking device indicated that Frank Thompson was on the move. Buster asked for the microphone so he could communicate with Thompson.

"Admiral, this is Buster. We are going to attempt a prisoner swap. Joe Monahan has volunteered. As soon as the swap is complete and you're in our custody, hit the dirt because all hell is going to break loose. If you understand me, just grunt twice."

Thompson indicated that he understood.

Buster then grabbed the loudspeaker microphone again and offered something more substantive than an order to lay down arms.

"We have in our custody Joseph Monahan, known to you as Abu Hussein. We propose to surrender Hussein to you in exchange for Admiral Thompson."

The front storm door of the house opened, the door banging against the wall as it was kicked open from inside.

Admiral Thompson appeared on the front porch, his face barely recognizable it was so bruised and swollen. Behind him was a man holding an AK-47 to Thompson's head.

CHAPTER SIXTY FOUR

What have they done to my Frankie, I thought as I looked at his beaten face. No, no, no. Stop the shit. This is just a mission, nothing more, nothing less. My job is to hit a target, a small target but bigger than thousands I've shot before. This is simply a task, and I have a Sig P210 to help me accomplish it. No anger, no hatred, no fear. Just hit the target.

I crouched with my Sig extended across the van's engine hood. I could see Frank's face clearly in my site.

"Buster," I said softly, "please tell Frank to move his head to the left, *his* left."

"Janice," Buster whispered loudly, "are you crazy?"

"Buster, Hon, you've seen me shoot before. I've got it. I've got the shot. I *own* this shot. Please ask Frank to move his head."

Buster talked into the microphone to Frank, asking him to move his head to his left.

It's just a mission, just a task, that's all it is. Hit the target, simple as that.

Frank moved his head slowly to his left. In a moment his captor's face was exposed.

I squeezed the trigger. The bullet screamed from the muzzle of the Sig, barely giving the gun a kick, which is why Sigs are so great for accuracy.

My bullet hit the middle of the target. The man fell, as did Frank.

Buster yelled a command into his microphone. The sound of at least twelve concussion grenades shook the neighborhood.

I looked at Frank's crumpled body and decided to go rogue. I ran to his side, almost tripping over Buster's high top sneakers. I unholstered my Glock G42. I was inclined to drop down and hold Frank, but the better part of my brain ordered me to crouch and hold my weapon in front of me. This is a mission, a simple fucking mission. I'm not angry, I'm not full of hate, and I'VE ABSOLUTELY TOTALLY GOT MY SHIT TOGETHER! *Stop, stop, calm down, focus.*

Out of the corner of my left eye I saw a short man in a helmet charging toward me. Charging me! The man lowered his shoulder and collided with my upper left arm, sending me flying about three feet to the dirt. I spun my head to see who this nut was, and there was Bennie, crouched next to Frank and emptying a clip from his Glock at the roof of the house. Two men fell to the yard.

"Secure the building and report," yelled Buster into his mike. The concussion grenades, not to mention Bennie, had done their work. All of the occupants, including Abbas Haddad, were dead.

I holstered my Glock, ran to Frank, and held his head in my hands. I kissed him on the only part of his face that wasn't bathed in blood.

"Ah buh vu," said Frank.

"Sorry, Frank, what was that?"

"AH...BUH...VU," he repeated through his broken jaw and swollen lips.

"I love you too, Honey."

CHAPTER SIXTY FIVE

Bennie and three paramedics came to Frank's side.
"Shove over, Kiddo," Bennie said to me.

I had forgotten that Bennie is not only a shrink but a medical doctor. While making notes on a voice recorder, Bennie went through a quick diagnosis of Frank's condition.

"Vitals look good, amazingly good. Jaw is cracked in at least two places. Nose is fractured. At least two fractured ribs. Heavy abrasions and facial tissue edema. No apparent fracturing to the orbital sockets. Frank, I need to go through some neurological stuff. Can you wiggle your toes? Great. Now squeeze my hand. Super. Now I'm going to check your limbs. Let me know when you feel pain."

Bennie continued to squeeze and poke every part of Frank's body. He then grabbed one of Frank's hands and one of mine.

"I'll take my miracles when I can get them," said Bennie. "Frank's in excellent shape even though he looks like shit."

He looked around to make sure the paramedics were out of earshot. Bennie winked and said, "You two should be ready to hop into the sack in two weeks, three max."

I could see Frank trying to wink at me, but it didn't work. So I winked at him.

⤜⟊ ⟊⤛

As Frank's gurney was wheeled to the ambulance, I walked over to Buster.

"I'm sorry, Buster. I know I shouldn't have run to Frank after I popped that guy."

"Janice, under the circumstances I would have done the same thing. You are one tough civilian broad. I can't believe you put that bullet right through the middle of the target. You owe me no apologies. I'll serve with you anytime and anywhere. Which reminds me, be in the Director's office at 4 PM sharp for a meeting."

"Yes, Sir."

CHAPTER SIXTY SIX

The hospital where Frank was headed was near CIA headquarters. Ben and I were in the ambulance with Frank. It felt good just to sit and take a breather, if only for a few minutes. I rested my feet on a trunk, admiring my size-12 high top Converse All Star basketball sneakers.

"Bennie, I have a request."

"What is it, Janice?"

"The next time you save my life, please be a little more gentle."

Bennie laughed and delivered a good natured buddy punch to my left arm. I winced in pain.

"Ouch, sorry Kiddo."

After we got to the hospital, Bennie convinced me that our hanging around didn't make sense because Frank would be heavily sedated and in need of rest.

"I have a 4 PM meeting with Buster and Carlini," I said, "about two hours from now. I assume you'll be there, yes?"

"Yes. I think Buster got some interesting news from Carlini while we were securing the safe house. He seemed really excited."

"Buster's always excited about something," I said.

CHAPTER SIXTY SEVEN

This morning was the second time I've killed a person. The first time was in Yemen, when I shot a crazy gunman who was about to mow down a restaurant full of people. Killing him was completely justified, but it still bothers me. This morning was different. When I put a bullet through that scumbag's head it felt good. It still feels good. I know that sounds heartless, but the man I shot was heartless. He tortured the man I love. The guy put himself in harm's way and I brought him harm. Frank taught me to focus on a mission and I did just that. If you ever point a gun at Frankie in my presence, make sure I'm unarmed.

There's something about a day full of gunfire, dirt, blood, and death that makes a shower feel extra good. I could really use a workout, but I can't be late for the meeting. The clock says I only have 20 minutes. Damn, no time to dry my hair. Maybe I'll wear my helmet to the meeting.

Bill Carlini called the meeting to order promptly at 4 PM. Buster's obsessiveness was starting to wear off on him.

Besides myself and Bennie, present at the meeting was Buster, Carlini, and, to my surprise, Joe Monahan.

"Bennie, I never realized you were such a masterful negotiator," said Buster, chuckling.

"A Glock with a full clip can be an excellent negotiating tool," said Bennie

"Okay, folks, things appear to be coming together," said Carlini. "This morning's rescue operation was an amazing display of courage and efficiency. It was also a typical Buster operation. We've got a lot to be happy about, not the least of which is that our friend Admiral Frank is okay and on the mend. Also, Abbas Haddad, probably the most evil sadistic terrorist on the planet, is dead, thanks to sharp-shooting Janice over here."

I lifted my towel covered head and said, "What?"

"I forgot to tell you, Janice," said Buster. "The guy you shot was Haddad himself."

Strange, but I felt like a prom queen as everyone politely applauded me. "Hey, let's hear it for the killer." Maybe I can have Haddad's head mounted and hung over my fireplace. I've got to stop this shit. I'm getting weird.

"I've asked Joe Monahan to join us for a couple of reasons," said Carlini. "First I want to thank Joe for his courage by offering himself as a prisoner swap for Frank. It didn't have to happen, as we all know, but Joe showed bravery that probably would have gotten him killed. I also want Joe's input on a matter I'll discuss next."

—✦ ✦—

"So here's some great news, folks," Carlini said. "A New York City cop positively identified the Ajax Plumbing Supply van this morning in lower Manhattan. He planted a bug, and it's under surveillance. The van hasn't moved since he found it. Here are some photos the cop took. Any recollection of it now, Joe?"

"Not a clue. But I'm glad Doctor Ben's hypnosis helped drag it out of me."

"So here's where we are," continued the Director. "We're making assumptions, but they're based on solid facts. We know the bombs were transferred from a freighter to a yacht named *Andiamo*. We first spotted *Andiamo* off northern Manhattan near the George Washington Bridge, so we assumed it had dropped off one of the bombs before that. Thanks to Bennie and Joe Monahan's subconscious recollection, we narrowed the first bomb to a plumbing supply van, which we've located. That makes five bombs, and we know where they are. It's now a question of disabling the bombs before anybody sets a timer. We're already working on the logistics of that operation. Does anybody have any thoughts or questions?"

I raised my hand, because I had a big question.

"Sheik Janice?" said Carlini.

Everybody laughed at Carlini's crack.

"I guess you're referring to my stylish head gear," I said. "Sorry, guys, it's been a busy day and I had no time to dry my hair. But I do have a question, Mr. Director, a big one. Because Sheik Haddad and his pals are presumably frolicking with their allocation of 72 virgins each, it seems that we've decapitated al Qaeda, or at least the leadership of this operation. Do we have any idea who the replacement management is, and more importantly, is there something sacred about the exact timing of the bombs, is there something immoveable about Thanksgiving day?"

"I'm in love with this woman," shouted Buster as he slammed his hands on the table. "If I weren't happily married and if Janice wasn't in love with Frank I'd offer her my hand in marriage right now."

We all laughed at Buster's charming compliment.

"Janice has nailed it. When will the attacks occur? That's not only *a* question, it's *the* question. We've got to attack and neutralize the bombs now. Joe Monahan, do you have any thoughts on the subject?"

"Symbolism is important to terrorism, the whole idea of which is to instill fear and also to change people's activities. Think of how the world's behavior changed after 9/11. Metal detectors, suitcase searches, full body scans. All that came about from a series of attacks on one day. The upcoming Thanksgiving Attacks are no different. The day of Thanksgiving has a huge symbolic meaning in the United States as a day of family and friendship. Al Qaeda's goal is to change that. But after this morning's operation I think that Thanksgiving may be a moveable feast, not to pun. Al Qaeda knows that the wraps are off this operation. Setting the bombs off on Thanksgiving Day would be a public relations coup, but I don't think it's critical to the operation. Buster's right, in my opinion. We've got to move now."

⚒

"Buster," said Carlini, "any operational thoughts?"

"Yes sir, and here they are. First the van in lower Manhattan. We need to get radiological detection equipment next to it as soon as possible to make sure the bomb's actually in the vehicle. We can assume that the van is booby trapped, so once we determine if the bomb is there we need to get in without an explosion."

"How soon can that happen, Buster?" asked Carlini.

"The detection device will be there in about 15 minutes. An ordnance disposal team from the NYPD is on alert and ready to move once they get instructions. We don't know where the bad guys are, so we have to be sensitive about messing with the van. If we determine that it's safe, we don't want some guy shooting a rocket-propelled grenade at it from a window."

"If I may," said Joe Monahan. "A nuclear trigger is always a traditional explosive that's used to start the chain reaction. But I know for certain that these bombs are set to go off with timers that will trip the first explosion. You may want to check what I'm saying with a nuclear engineer, but I don't think that there can be a nuclear explosion without the timing device; otherwise the bombs would be too sensitive for moving around. I agree that the van is probably booby trapped, but I don't think that it could trigger a nuclear explosion. Also, consider the possibility that the van is *not* booby trapped. Why would al Qaeda risk an entire operation just because some kid tried to carjack the vehicle?"

"Excellent points, Joe," said Buster. "The NYPD had some of the best experts in the world for detecting explosives. I'm confident that we'll know if it's booby trapped before we try to break into it. We'll know soon."

"Next," continued Buster, "let's address the yacht *Andiamo*. Right now it's cruising near Ossining, New York. I've checked and found out that the boat is equipped with excellent radar. That means that a drone would trigger an alarm if it got too close. The yacht is moving slowly. Our guess is that it's trying to conserve fuel and avoid a refueling stop. Our current thinking is that we use an aircraft, maybe a good old A-10 Warthog. They can fly slow or fast and they carry the punch of an army tank. We can use the A-10 to shoot tear gas canisters through an upper window. Because tear gas is heavier than air, the gas will seep below to all compartments and immobilize whoever's on board. We then board the yacht and stabilize it, shooting whoever we need to. SEALs are great at securing vessels both large and small. I'm in communication with the commanding officer of the SEAL team in Little Creek, Virginia. They're already on the move."

"With your permission, Sir, I'll make these plans operational right now," Buster said to Carlini.

"Buster, I long ago abandoned any idea of slowing you down. Go for it, my friend."

CHAPTER SIXTY EIGHT

Bennie Weinberg here.

What a fucking day this has been, if you'll pardon my bluntness. Me, Bennie the Shrink – in combat! I've written a few books, but now I have enough book material that I don't think I'll live long enough to write them all. I'm surrounded by amazing people, really great people, most especially Buster the spook and the brave and gutsy Janice Monahan. I feel good about today. I never shot a man before, but today I shot two. I don't feel bad about it because they were about to kill my friend Janice, not to mention her wounded boyfriend, Admiral Frank. Come to think of it, they were probably targeting yours truly as well. If there's one thing I'm glad I've done over the years, it was maintaining my proficiency on the shooting range.

But tonight, I get to relax for a few short hours in the beautiful cafeteria of the Central Intelligence Agency. I even have a date, my former girlfriend Maggie Cohen, a woman I'm planning on making my current girlfriend.

"Bennie, is that a friggin' bruise on your face?" asked Maggie.

"I had an interesting morning, Maggie, quite an interesting morning."

I hate when people play coy with me and only hint at stories, so I told Maggie all about our morning shootout. I'm not sure she had a "need to know," but she has Top Secret clearance and I thought she should be aware of what was going on. As one of the country's top experts on the Middle East, maybe she can help me figure out these nut job al Qaeda types.

"So, besides acting like a middle aged cowboy, how is the bomb hunt going Bennie?"

"You know, Mag, I realize you've got Top Secret clearance and all that, but that part of the operation is at a sensitive stage so I don't think I should go there. Let's just say we're working on it. Your boss Buster is in charge of the mission, and that fact alone gives me confidence. Let's just leave it at that."

Maggie's a pro. She got it immediately and took no offense. Thank God for that. The last person I'd want to offend was this pretty redhead.

"Maggie, help me to understand something. I'm as well-read as the next guy, but I'm having the damnedest time understanding what these radical Islamists are up to. This morning I was involved in a gun battle with 12 guys who wanted nothing more than to kill us. Sure we killed them, but that wasn't our objective. We were there to free a kidnapped man, which we did, thank God. But all they want to do is kill us, as well as a few million other people in a few weeks. Help me understand this Maggie. You're the expert."

"Bennie, I've been studying the Middle East for most of my adult life. Yeah, they call me an expert, and I get to play the maven on occasional Sunday morning talk shows. But just like this crazy time travel stuff you people seem so fond of, I remain stumped by most of what's been going on for the past few centuries. I can tell you that the Shiites and Sunni Muslims have been at each other's throats since the Seventh Century. They're still fighting over who is the rightful heir to the Prophet Mohammed. That's right, to this day, 1,400 years later, they're still killing one another over that issue. And when they're not slaughtering each other, they train their sights on us, the Infidels, especially us Jews. I understand it, I teach it, I've written books about it, but I still don't get it. The change, if it ever happens, will come from within, from some leader who steps forward and blows the whistle and announces that it's time to move on. But that guy is not on the horizon. Meanwhile, we all try to keep it together and stop our civilization from being destroyed."

Maggie gave me a wan smile and squeezed my hand.

"Does that clear it all up, Ben?"

"Why don't we find a more pleasant subject to talk about," I said. "How about you and me?"

Unlike me, Professor Maggie does not suffer from introversion. She stood up, walked quickly around the table, and planted a deep kiss on my lips.

I think Mom will love this lady

CHAPTER SIXTY NINE

Jack Thurber here.

30 minutes ago I was at work. Now I'm walking into the office of the Director of the Central Intelligence Agency. Everybody calls me a time traveler. Whenever I deal with Buster I find that time just takes on another dimension. Buster, I think, is a human wormhole.

I sat down next to Buster in front of Carlini's desk. I'm looking for a good way to describe the look on both of their faces. I think "bedraggled" fits the bill.

"Jack," said Carlini, "I'm renewing your charter membership in The Thanksgiving Gang. To understate the obvious, things are heating up."

"I realize that," I said. "I spoke to Ashley this morning. She told me she sank three ships yesterday, not something she does on a typical weekday." I was trying to introduce a bit of levity to ease the tension.

They didn't think I was funny.

"Here's the bottom line, Jack. I received a call from the White House, from the President himself. Our country is going through a series of events that we've never seen before, a series of crises that we only know about because of a guy we all call the *Time Magnet*. That, of course, would be you, my friend. The President wants all of this chronicled for the history books. He said he can't think of a better man for the job than you, and I agree with him. You not only have this proclivity for tripping through wormholes, you're also a Pulitzer Prize winner and one of the best journalists in the business."

"Will I still keep my status as a provisional deputy CIA agent?"

"Yes, you will," said Buster. "I know you think that's a conflict of interest, but strange times call for strange procedures. Everything you write, because of your imbedded status and a Top Secret clearance, will be vetted by the CIA. I know you hate that idea, but national security demands it. We want you to be completely candid in your writing, and only sensitive active intelligence information will be redacted. In your opening paragraphs you'll disclose your status with the CIA. Let future historians sort that stuff out. We don't doubt that the chronicles you prepare will eventually turn into a book. That's fine, and actually that's what the President wants. The book will bear your copyright and all advances and royalties will be yours. You're a wealthy man who will soon become a lot wealthier. Any questions, Jack?"

"I can't turn this down," I said. "I don't like the idea of agreeing up front to giving the CIA the first right of review, but I understand. These are strange and different times. I have to say I'm flattered."

"Jack," said Carlini, "I flatter Buster over here all the time, for one reason. He deserves it. And so do you. So let's give history something to sink its teeth into. Maybe some future historian, working with your book as a starting place, can figure all this shit out. I sure as hell can't."

"That makes two of us, Mr. Director."

"Make it three," said Buster.

CHAPTER SEVENTY

I'm sitting next to Frank's bed in the hospital. Buster allowed me to leave Agency Headquarters on the condition that I wear a disguise. I took off my burqa after I entered the room. Frank is fast asleep, which is okay with me. I'm content just to sit here and hold his hand, my brain drenched in the happy thought that he's alive.

It's been just over 48 hours since the gunfight and Frank's rescue from the al Qaeda safe house. Although he's still extremely bruised, his facial swelling, or edema as Bennie put it, has gone down.

He began to wake up. He looked at me and squeezed my hand. With my knack for focusing on irrelevant things, I commented that the coffee burn on the back of his hand looked a lot better.

Frank laughed, then held out his hand and winced, as if to say, "Please, do not make me laugh."

Frank's jaw was still wired shut, but, because his lip swelling had gone down, he was able to form words, even though he had to speak through clenched teeth.

"I've never loved anyone as much as I love you, Honey," Frank said, sounding like Al Pacino in *The Godfather* in the scene after his jaw was broken.

I kissed him on his forehead.

"I love you too, more than you'll ever know," I said.

"Well, I think I have a pretty good idea," Frank said slowly. "I knew you loved me, but when you risked your life to save mine, I believe that qualifies as true love."

I wanted to hug him, but he'd need anesthesia for me to do that, so I just kept stroking his hand, the one without the coffee burn.

"I followed your orders, Admiral Frankie. I showed up at the safe house without anger, hatred, or fear. I was heavily armed, but I kept my emotions to myself and focused on the mission."

"And you put a bullet through a small target from a distance of 30 yards," said Frank. "When I feel better I want you to take me out skeet shooting. You can teach me a thing or two."

Dolores, the nurse, put her head in the door.

"Dr. Carleton says the Admiral needs as much rest as possible, Janice."

"No problem, Dolores, I'm leaving shortly."

"So, Frank, you're not going to sea anytime soon, I guess."

"No, they've already appointed my old friend Bill Schweitzer to head the Strike Group. I can't very well give commands through clenched teeth."

"The important thing is that you get better. I can't wait to be with you. I think I'll slip into a sexy little thing like my quadruple size United States Naval Academy bathrobe."

Frank started laughing, again putting his hand out to ask me to stop. I can't believe I'm inflicting pain on the man I love with my dumb jokes.

CHAPTER SEVENTY ONE

Among the dangerous tasks a Navy SEAL learns, securing a building is one of them. At 9 PM on November 4, a team of 12 SEALs were dropped off behind a building on Bleecker Street in the Greenwich Village neighborhood of Manhattan. They were accompanied by two FBI agents. Unlike Chicago, New York City does not have utility alleyways running behind buildings. New York City real estate is too expensive to allow for such conveniences. But the two buildings on either side of the Ajax Plumbing van were once factories and had small yards in back for loading and unloading deliveries. This stroke of luck would enable the SEALs to break in from the rear if they needed to. The tenant status of both buildings had already been checked out by the NYPD. There were commercial renters on the first two floors and residential tenants on the next two. Each building was only four stories in height. The only windows were on the upper two floors, the residential units. Of the eight residential tenants, only one had been occupied recently, three days before. The tenants had Middle Eastern names, which normally would not raise eyebrows. But SEALs knew, as any trained military or law enforcement professional learned, the best plan is to go for the most obvious – concentrate on the new residential tenants. The SEALs had a search warrant from the Foreign Intelligence Surveillance Court, enabling them to break the door down if needed.

With four SEALs at his side, FBI agent Marcus Crowley knocked on the door and yelled, "FBI, open the door immediately."

He repeated his demand in Arabic.

No response.

Two SEALs swung a battering ram against the door which knocked it off its hinges. The five entered the apartment with guns drawn. As one SEAL entered a bedroom a shot rang out, hitting him harmlessly in his Kevlar vest, but not without inflicting a stabbing pain. The SEAL behind him opened fire, killing the shooter. They saw another occupant opening a window. Next to him was a rope ladder, apparently in place for an occasion such as this. Two SEALs wrestled the man to the floor, handcuffing him. The man screamed in Arabic.

As the SEALs secured the apartment, making sure there was no one else present, FBI agent Crowley searched the rooms. In one room alone he found six AK-47 rifles, twelve 45-caliber handguns, and 10 hand grenades.

Crowley then looked out the window. The Ajax Plumbing van was three stories beneath him, still parked in the alley.

"Great work, guys," said Crowley. "Ours was the easy part. It's now up to the bomb disposal folks."

CHAPTER SEVENTY TWO

Detective Lieutenant James Mulrooney, the man in command of the NYPD Bomb Disposal Unit, had just been briefed by the CIA on the task before him and his team. They were to investigate a vehicle near Bleecker Street in Lower Manhattan, a burgundy van marked Ajax Plumbing Supply. Mulrooney had been through this procedure so many times it was almost second nature to him. But he always avoided complacency, a lapse in attention that could get him killed. There is never anything second nature about a booby trap.

But this briefing was different. The briefing officer told him that he was about to engage in the most dangerous assignment he ever faced in his 18 years on the force. He and his people were about to check out a vehicle for explosives, a vehicle that may contain a nuclear bomb.

The first job was to determine if the van actually contained nuclear materials. A radiological detection device was slowly wheeled around the van. In less than a minute, Mulrooney had the confirmation he was looking for. Yes, the van contained nuclear materials.

Now comes the scary part, thought Mulrooney. Using a newly patented explosives detection instrument, Mulrooney and one of his men went over every inch of the van, slowly, painstakingly slowly, trying to detect evidence of a booby trap. After 30 minutes, Mulrooney determined that the van was free of an explosive device. He knew that a booby trap can consist of mechanisms that don't use explosives, devices that spring open and hurl projectiles at an intruder. But the bomb armor or bomb suits that the team wore, he figured, were ample protection against a mechanically triggered projectile.

He had been trained where to look for the timing mechanism. He found it and exhaled. The timer had not yet been set.

The van, which contained a 10-kiloton nuclear bomb, was secure. The vehicle was then rolled up a ramp onto the top of a flat bed truck, which slowly drove out onto Bleecker Street. An escort of 12 police cars awaited. Next stop was Rodman's Neck in the borough of the Bronx, a 54-acre NYPD facility used for weapons training. The facility could do nothing to contain a 10-kiloton nuclear blast, but it would serve as a temporary location until further instructions.

Lower Manhattan, at least, was safe.

CHAPTER SEVENTY THREE

B en and I were in Director Carlini's office for what Buster promised would be a short meeting. I brought everyone up to date on
Frank's health, having visited him at the hospital that morning.

"This is going to be a short meeting," said Buster, "because we're
about to move out, fast. I've given you the great news about the Ajax
Plumbing van bomb. It's secured and at a safe location. The subject
of this meeting is our next target, the yacht *Andiamo*. As you know,
our intelligence tells us that she's carrying the four remaining nukes.
The NYPD secured the vehicle in lower Manhattan, but we have to assume that the occupants of *Andiamo* know there's a problem because
the van people aren't answering their cellphones. The men we killed
at the safe house where Admiral Frank was held won't be answering their phones either. We're going to hit *Andiamo* fast and hard, as
hard as we can, knowing she's packing nuclear bombs. A Navy SEAL
team of 18 men is waiting for us at West Point, where *Andiamo* will
soon pass. At West Point, we'll board a 67-foot yacht named, *White
Cloud*, presumably after the product that her former owner traded in
until we locked him up and seized the ship. He was a cocaine dealer.

We're using a civilian yacht rather than a military vessel because we don't want to announce any intentions to the people on *Andiamo*. The SEALs will then swarm aboard and drop enough tear gas canisters to disable a herd of elephants. I've given up the idea of using an A-10 to shoot the canisters at the ship. We need boots on the dock. Tear gas is heavier than air, so it should seep into every compartment and do the trick. Then we secure the nukes and be on our way."

"Ben will be with us to help with interrogations if we take any live prisoners," Buster continued. "Janice you'll stay here at Langley. I know from personal experience that you're one tough combat veteran, but we won't need your sharpshooting skills on this mission, not with 18 SEALs."

"But I'll be your most important team member, Buster. You have to take me with you."

"Janice, you're the best. I'd have you covering my back any time. But there's just no reason to put you in harm's way for this operation."

"Hold on, Buster," said Carlini. "I want to hear why Janice thinks she's needed. Janice, please go on."

"I can deliver the tear gas in a much better way than you've outlined," I said. "I once designed the air conditioning system for a *Feadship* yacht. They have scuppers all over the deck."

"What's a scupper?" asked Bennie.

"A scupper is an air intake device. It looks something like an inverted gramophone. The purpose is to bring in fresh air and distribute it throughout the yacht. They have filters, but they're pretty broad gauge, meant to catch bird shit and feathers. The filters won't stop tear gas. Assuming the ship is well maintained, and yachts like that usually are, the filters should be clean as a whistle, but even if they're partially clogged, tear gas will get through. So rather than have the entire platoon of SEALs running around and getting shot at, we assign maybe six of them to run onto the deck and drop gas canisters into the scuppers. One team should be tasked to secure the bridge.

Once that's done, just turn off the air conditioning and hit the "out-side air" switch, which will suck air throughout the system. The ship will be choking in tear gas in no time."

"Are you familiar with large boats like this, other than their air conditioning systems?" asked Buster.

"Sure," I said. "I'm licensed as a captain by the U.S. Coast Guard to operate vessels up to 100 tons. I took the course for fun, just because I love boating, but it really comes in handy, as in an operation like this."

Buster and Bennie just looked at me and shook their heads.

"Janice," said Carlini, "when you return I want to have a long conversation with you about your future career plans."

"Okay, gang," said Buster. "Let's move out. We have a helicopter waiting for us."

CHAPTER SEVENTY FOUR

W est Point, the home of the United States Military Academy, is not a maritime facility but it has docking along the Hudson River, more than adequate for our needs. Buster also chose West Point for obvious security purposes.

The yacht *White Cloud*, formerly the property of a drug king pin, is a sharp-looking well- appointed 67-foot vessel. We boarded at 11:30 AM in a gentle early November breeze with the temperature about 60 degrees. While the crew made plans to get underway, I took Buster, Bennie, and Lieutenant John Billings, the man in charge of the SEAL detachment, on a tour of the boat's scuppers. We then went to the bridge so I could show them the air intake switch.

Captain Wayne Cropsey, CIA retired, was in charge of the vessel. A big man in every way, maybe 6-feet, 4-inches, he was also extremely overweight. Buster introduced all of us to Cropsey, who eagerly thrust out his hand. He seemed so proud and pleased you would have thought the yacht was his.

"I love being a spook temp," said Cropsey. "When I get done with a job, I go back down to Florida where I skipper my own boat.

So it seems like we've got a sensitive as hell operation going on, Buster."

Before Buster could respond, Cropsey went into a hacking, coughing fit.

"Sorry, folks," said Cropsey. "Damn Northern weather."

Bennie noted to me in a whisper that it was 60 degrees and sunny.

"I'm just showing these guys a few switches, Captain Wayne," I said.

"If I can help let me know, but I've only been aboard for a couple of days," said Cropsey.

I showed them the air conditioning switch and the fresh air intake.

"I wish I had a diagram of the bridge on *Andiamo*," I said. "That would make a picture worth a thousand words."

"Oh, I have that," said Buster.

He reached into his briefcase and pulled out a manual that he had downloaded from the Feadship Manufacturing site.

"Were you saving this for Christmas, Buster?" I asked, a little miffed.

"Sorry," Buster said. "I didn't think about it."

It's rare that Buster doesn't think of everything, so I let it go.

"You've seen the scuppers, Lieutenant. They'll be easy to spot on *Andiamo* as well."

I spread the cabin diagram out on the navigation table and immediately spotted the fresh air intake switch.

"When you select your scupper team, Lieutenant," I said, "I suggest that you assign a special team to the bridge so they know where to find the switch. It will make your day a hell of a lot easier than racing around the ship throwing tear gas canisters."

Captain Cropsey walked over to the console.

"Notice the 'whooshing' sound when you throw the fresh air intake," said Cropsey, helpfully. "You won't have to guess if you hit the right one."

A woman who I didn't know entered the bridge.

"Molly, great to see you," said Buster.

Molly MacDevitt was a petite thin woman, I'd say about 55 years old. She had thick gray hair, pulled back into a pony tail.

"Professor Molly MacDevitt is a nuclear physicist from Cal Tech. She's also with the Nuclear Regulatory Commission. Molly's here to oversee the stabilizing of the bombs once we've secured *Andiamo*. Her specialty is nuclear weapons."

"You must be a lot of fun at a cocktail party," said Bennie.

Molly let out a loud laugh.

"Yes, and my jokes never bomb," said Molly, as she gave Bennie a high five.

A nuclear bomb expert with a sense of humor. Our operation needs a person like this, I thought.

With that, Cropsey fell into another hacking, coughing fit. Bennie caught my eye. We both raised our eyebrows.

As we were leaving the bridge, Bennie pulled me over just outside the doorway.

"Hey, Kiddo. Is that captain's license of yours up to date?"

My eyes widened and I just nodded. Bennie had just posed an important question. We could hear Captain Cropsey coughing as the door closed.

Buster walked over to Bennie and me. He leaned close.

"Janice, I have a question."

"I'm gonna guess it's the one Ben just asked me. Yes, my captain's license is current. I can drive this thing."

"Janice, the bridge is your duty station until further notice. Keep your eyes on that guy."

"Yes, sir." I said.

I was about to make that suggestion.

CHAPTER SEVENTY FIVE

We cast off lines and got underway at 2:30 PM. It was November 5, just shy of three weeks to Thanksgiving. I think Buster got it right as usual. We shouldn't look at Thanksgiving as the set date for the attacks. We're operating under the assumption that the plan could go into effect at any time. Although we don't know anything about *Andiamo*'s drop-off plans, we assume that there will be a delivery to one or more land vehicles to transport the bombs to targets across the country. The guess is that *Andiamo* will head toward the St. Lawrence Seaway and proceed into the Great Lakes where it can connect with shore vehicles. That's the guess, but *Andiamo*'s destination is almost irrelevant. We're getting ready to launch our own attack.

As Buster ordered, I was on the bridge with Captain Cropsey, who seemed to have non-stop coughing fits.

"I appreciate Buster giving me a purdy gal to look at while I'm on the job," said Cropsey.

Stuff it, Bozo, I thought.

"You just concentrate on the instruments and our course, Wayne. I'll be here to help in any way you need."

"Well I hear tell that you're a licensed captain, pretty lady, so why don't you take the helm while I go outside and have a smoke."

Great. Overweight, coughing like a kennel dog, and now he wants a cigarette.

"I got the helm, Wayne," I said. "Enjoy your smoke."

We steered a course that would bring us within visual contact of *Andiamo* within an hour. The bomb yacht was travelling at a slow speed, probably to save on fuel. According to our radar and GPS, *Andiamo* was doing only five knots, the speed of a vessel entering or leaving a marina.

Captain Cropsey came back into the cabin after his tobacco break, coughing more than usual. I noticed that he was sweating profusely, even though the temperature was a comfortable 60 degrees. I also noticed that he kept rubbing his left arm.

"I'll take over, pretty gal."

"The name's Janice, Wayne," I said. If I don't call him fatso, he should reciprocate by using my real name.

I was on the port side of the bridge, familiarizing myself with the various dials and instrument displays. I heard a loud thud. I looked at Cropsey but he wasn't there. I then looked at the deck, and there he was, flat on his back and apparently unconscious.

"This is the bridge," I shouted into the microphone. "Man down, man down, man down on the bridge. Need medical assistance." I didn't know if that's what I was supposed to say, but it seemed natural.

In moments a SEAL corpsman ran onto the bridge with his medical bag. Doctor Bennie was right behind him. The corpsman felt Cropsey's neck for a pulse. There wasn't any.

"This poor guy's dead," the corpsman announced.

Buster came running through the door. He looked at Cropsey, then at Bennie, who just shook his head. Then Buster looked at me.

"Captain Janice, you're in command of this vessel."

I felt nervous. I'd skippered larger yachts than this, and frankly I felt more confident with me than with our poor deceased colleague at the helm. But I was nervous because we were soon to engage in a violent military operation, an operation that would decide the future of the country. I kept reminding myself of Frank's advice. Focus on the mission, nothing else.

The fact that I was scared shitless is totally irrelevant.

CHAPTER SEVENTY SIX

B uster called a pre-attack briefing on the bridge. Lieutenant
Billings, the SEAL commanding officer was there, along with
SEAL Chief Petty Officer Jay Filippo, and two other SEALs. Our nuclear physicist friend Molly MacDevitt was also there, along with me
and Bennie. The bridge was spacious enough to accommodate the
meeting.

"Right now it's 3:45 PM," said Buster, "or 1545 for our military
friends. Sunset is at 4:49, about an hour from now. As Lieutenant
Billings reminds me, the SEALs own the night, and we will attack at
7:30 PM under cover of total darkness. I'm going to turn this over to
Lt. Billings to brief us on the plan."

⬤⬤ ⬤⬤

"Our objective is to neutralize all personnel aboard *Andiamo,* and
then to secure four nuclear bombs," said Billings. "If it weren't for
the nukes, our operation would be routine. We've trained more than
I can remember on how to attack and neutralize a large boat. The

218

nukes present some interesting complications, but Captain Janice over here has come up with an excellent plan to drop tear gas canisters into the yacht's scuppers."

"Do we have any idea where the bombs are located, Lieutenant?" asked Molly.

"We don't have a clue, professor," said Billings. "Our plan is to incapacitate the onboard personnel and to leave the nukes in your capable hands."

"I can't wait," said Professor Molly with a chuckle as she rubbed her hands together. We had all taken a liking to this lady.

"As we slowly come up on the target's port side," said Billings, "we'll launch three Zodiac inflatable boats over *our* port side so they won't be seen until the final moments. Each Zodiac will carry four SEALs making a total boarding party of twelve men. Four guys are tasked to drop the canisters in the scuppers, two on the port side and two on starboard. Four men will storm the bridge, as Captain Janice has recommended, to hit the air intake switches and suck the gas throughout the ship. Within a couple of minutes the air on *Andiamo* won't be breathable. Four SEALs will remain on this vessel on the upper deck for sniper duty in case any bad guys make it to an outside deck on *Andiamo*. I don't expect much gunfire, but we're ready for it. After stinging eyes and a lung full of tear gas, the enemy will be temporarily retired from the gun shooting business. Anybody who boards *Andiamo* will have an oxygen breathing apparatus.

"Captain Janice will then transfer from *White Cloud* to *Andiamo* after we've neutralized the ship. We had a captain scheduled to be brought in by helicopter, but Buster and I decided that Janice has the expertise we need for this operation. One of my guys knows how to operate a boat and he'll stay here to run the *White Cloud*. At that point there should be little to do until a Navy ship comes alongside with a nuclear weapons team to help Professor MacDevitt with the bombs."

"I hope they're young and handsome," said Molly.

I think Molly must have attended a Frank Thompson lecture on remaining calm under stress.

"So that's it, folks," said Buster. "We tear gas an 85-foot yacht, neutralizing the personnel aboard. Then Professor MacDevitt and the other experts do their thing with the nukes. After that we can all make our plans for a wonderful Thanksgiving."

CHAPTER SEVENTY SEVEN

At 7:30 PM, I maneuvered the *White Cloud* 100 feet abeam the port side of *Andiamo*. We wanted to appear to be just another boat passing in the same direction. The target yacht was still creeping along at five knots, and I set our speed at seven knots, just enough to edge ahead slowly. The SEALs launched the three Zodiacs and arrived at *Andiamo*'s large swim platform in moments. Two enemy men on *Andiamo* ran to the edge of the upper deck when they heard the whine of the Zodiacs' engines. SEAL snipers on *White Cloud* opened fire with silenced carbines, killing the men instantly. The tear gas team fanned out along the deck dropping the canisters into *Andiamo*'s scuppers.

Four SEALs stormed onto the bridge, shooting three of the four men on watch. Petty Officer Condon ran to the console and flipped on the fresh air intake switches to send the tear gas throughout the ship. One man, stationed at the helm, immediately raised his hands over his head and shouted, "I'm American!"

One of the SEALs opened all the windows on the bridge to disperse the tear gas.

Petty Officer Jackson, the man in charge of the bridge team, aimed his carbine at the man in front of the helm as I took over the operation of the ship. Looking at an array of dials and switches through a gas mask is a real trick.

Jackson led the man to the outside deck next to the bridge. As planned, Bennie showed up to aid in interrogation. Buster was with him. The man who I relieved at the helm had ingested only a small amount of tear gas, but he seemed to be in obvious distress.

"Listen to me, pal," said Bennie. "I know you want to take deep breaths but don't do it. Just gulp short shallow breaths and you'll feel fine shortly."

"What's your name?" asked Buster.

"My name's Mike McDonald," said the man as he gulped fresh air. "I was hired in Florida by these scumbags. They got my name off a 'Captain for Hire' bulletin board at the marina."

"Do you know how many men are aboard?" asked Buster.

"Twelve, including me."

"Great," said Lieutenant Billings. "All ship's personnel have been accounted for. Six dead, one captured, four remaining on deck one, plus Mike McDonald here makes 12."

"I assume you've been kept in the dark about what this ship is carrying," said Buster.

"No, they told me everything. I assumed they intended to kill me shortly so they didn't bother to keep any secrets. It seemed like they wanted to brag about what they were doing. LISTEN TO ME. We've already dropped off one bomb on the West Side of Manhattan."

"To a burgundy van marked Ajax Plumbing Supply?" asked Bennie.

"Yes," McDonald said. "You guys are on the game, I see."

"There's another thing you people have to know right away," said McDonald. "We're running low on fuel. I suggested that we top off the tanks a few times, but these assholes aren't exactly mariners. We were scheduled to stop at a fuel dock in Kingston, about a half-hour north of here."

"Do you know where the bombs are located on this ship?" asked Buster.

"Deck one, forward. There's a big lounge with a bar. The next compartment is a small theater with a viewing screen. These shit-heads have been watching porno movies since we left Florida. The next compartment forward is where they've stored the bombs."

Buster called Professor MacDevitt, who had just stepped onto the upper deck with her bomb team as he dialed. Buster described the bomb location to Molly.

Lieutenant Billings radioed his men on deck one to let them know the location of the bomb compartment, and to let them know that Professor MacDevitt and her team were on their way.

The SEALs on deck one ran through the lounge area and into the theater, where an orgy scene was playing on the screen. The four men in the audience, even though they were choking on tear gas, grabbed their AK-47s. The SEALs opened fire, killing them.

"The door's locked, Lieutenant," said one of the SEALs on deck one.

"Is that a woman I hear moaning?" asked Billings.

"We just interrupted a jihadi porn film festival, Sir. I turned it off."

Scumbags, thought McDonald.

"It's not a security lock," said McDonald. "They should be able to break the door down without using explosives."

"You copy that?" asked Billings over his phone.

The SEALs easily broke into the room and Professor MacDevitt and her team entered the bomb space. The bombs were all located along the forward bulkhead, heavily covered with blankets, which they began to remove.

※+ +※

"Oh Dear God Almighty," Molly screamed.

"One of the bombs is armed. The timer's set for three hours."

CHAPTER SEVENTY EIGHT

B uster announced Molly's horrifying discovery to all of us on the bridge.

"Mike," Buster yelled to *Andiamo*'s former captain. How far can we get with the fuel we have?"

"Ten miles, max. We need fuel now. Why not continue to the fuel dock I was headed for?"

"Wrong direction," said Buster. "We have to get this ship south into the open ocean."

"Mike, Janice, can you plot a course on the GPS and give me an ETA to a point, say, 25 miles southeast of the Verrazano Bridge?"

"You need more room than that, Buster," said Professor Molly, who had just stepped onto the bridge. "It's impossible. New York Harbor is roughly 75 miles from here." Molly had done the math in her head.

"Top speed on this thing is 20 knots," said McDonald, "but we can't make that speed if we have to stop or slow down to take on fuel. Even if we did make top speed we'd blow up half of Manhattan before we got anywhere near open ocean."

"A helicopter is the obvious way to go," said Buster.

"Agreed," said Professor Molly. "And we need to off load that bomb soon, real soon."

Buster called Director Carlini at the CIA and then called the White House. A CRH-60M combat/rescue helicopter took off from Stewart Air Force Base in nearby Newburgh within five minutes.

"Okay, folks, here's the drill," said Buster. "As Mike McDonald had intended, we're going to continue on to the fuel dock in Kingston. There we'll meet a helicopter from Stewart Air Force Base."

—⟨⟩—

Andiamo tied up to a fuel dock in Kingston. The helicopter was waiting.

Before she left the bridge, Molly turned to me, smiled and gave me a friendly pat on the shoulder.

"My parents wanted me to go into botany," Molly said.

Professor Molly MacDevitt, nuclear physicist, walked swiftly to the helicopter, her arm around the waist of a handsome young scientist from the Nuclear Regulatory Commission. The objective was to drop the bomb in deep water off the continental shelf beyond the end of the Hudson River Canyon, a deep trench that extends 400 miles southeast of New York City. Molly insisted that the weapon be dropped beyond the canyon to avoid the risk of creating a tsunami by crumbling the walls of the trench.

The date is November 5, 2015, three weeks to Thanksgiving.

CHAPTER SEVENTY NINE

The Washington Times

"Nuclear Bomb Attacks on Five American cities Thwarted – Timer on One Bomb Had Been Set – Disposed of at Sea – Helicopter Lost"

By Jack Thurber, November 6, 2015

A potential catastrophe of epic proportions was thwarted yesterday by the combined efforts of the Central Intelligence Agency, the Federal Bureau of Investigation, and the New York City Police Department.

A cell of al Qaeda, the international terrorist organization, planned to detonate five suitcase nuclear bombs in Chicago, Los Angeles, New York City, San Francisco, and Washington DC. The bombs were between 10 and 12-Kilotons in yield, each approximately the size of the atomic bomb dropped on Hiroshima in 1945. The original target date for the attacks was the upcoming Thanksgiving holiday, less than three weeks from now, but intelligence operations uncovered a plan to move the date forward.

The discovery of the planned attacks came a few days on the heels of another nuclear terrorist operation, the detonation of suitcase bombs on five American aircraft carriers. Those weapons were discovered and disposed of on October 17, just three weeks ago.

The weapons were transferred from the freighter *Sea Bounder*, a known smuggling ship, to a luxury yacht, the 85-foot *Andiamo*, off the south shore of Long Island three days ago. After delivering one bomb to a location in lower Manhattan, *Andiamo* continued its journey up the Hudson River, presumably headed to the St. Lawrence Seaway to deliver the other bombs to land based transportation. The Manhattan bomb was taken to a secure location. A team of 18 SEALs attacked the yacht last night with tear gas grenades and small arms. The battle was over in a matter of minutes. Of the 12 men aboard, only two survived, including Captain Mike McDonald, an American yacht captain who had been kidnapped and forced to operate the vessel. There were no SEAL injuries or deaths.

In a terrifying twist to the story, one of the bombs was armed and its timer set to detonate three hours after the SEALs secured the yacht. The weapon was transferred to an Air Force helicopter and dropped into the ocean off the continental shelf about 400 miles southwest of New York City.

Helicopter Lost

The story also includes a tragedy. The Air Force helicopter that carried nuclear bomb expert, Professor Molly MacDevitt, fell from the sky, apparently having been caught in the nuclear blast, even though the detonation occurred hundreds of feet below the ocean surface. According to an Air Force spokesman, Professor MacDevitt insisted that the helicopter wait until the last moments before releasing its deadly cargo in order to place the explosion as far from land as possible. The names of the other crewmembers of the helicopter have yet to be released, pending notification of next of kin. Professor MacDevitt is survived by her parents and two daughters.

The Civilian Deputies

The operation was assisted by a group of four civilians who were deputized as CIA agents. They called themselves The Thanksgiving Gang. For security reasons, their names have not been disclosed, nor have the names of the SEALs been made public.

How a nuclear attack on the United States could have come so close to fruition is a question that will linger into the months ahead, as a Congressional commission is sure to be empanelled. What could have been the largest disaster in American history came close to succeeding.

CHAPTER EIGHTY - BENNIE WEINBERG HERE

Bennie Weinberg here.

It's November 27, 2015, the day after Thanksgiving. Buster, as we all expected, wanted to exercise, as he put it, "an abundance of caution," so we all remained on duty throughout the holiday even though operation Tango Delta 2 was a success.

I'm here at my mom and dad's house in New Jersey along with, get this, my fiancée, the beautiful and brilliant Professor Maggie Cohen. I proposed to Maggie the day after the *Andiamo* operation. I wanted to wait until I was sure we'd all be alive for the foreseeable future. I'm not a terribly emotional guy, well at least not outwardly. But when Maggie accepted I thought I'd pass out for joy.

I'm supposed to feel happy, and well, I *am* happy. But, like detective Colombo used to say every week on TV, "Something's bothering me."

What a wonderful Thanksgiving, if a day late. We, meaning the Thanksgiving Gang and our circle of helpers, put our two cents in and prevented an unimaginable disaster. I've had good friends all my life, but never like these people. My good buddy Jack Thurber, Mr. Time Magnet himself, is reunited with his wife Captain Ashley Patterson. Janice Monahan, multitalented, beautiful, and tough as nails, is engaged to a wonderful guy, Admiral Frank Thompson. They expect to marry as soon as Janice's divorce decree becomes final. Joe Monahan, Janice's estranged husband, who we thought was a terrorist maggot a few short weeks ago, did a turnaround that spun our heads. We couldn't have done it without his help. I've heard a rumor that his sentence will be commuted. I hope the rumor's true. Wally Burton, a star *New York Times* reporter, put in everything he could for his country, and for us. Buster, the amazing and enigmatic CIA agent is on a well-deserved vacation. CIA Director Bill Carlini is rumored to be a possible pick as a vice-presidential candidate in the next election. A great guy, a calm leader, and a fine American. And then, of course, there's Maggie and me. It's not like I fell in love after a brief fling. I've known Maggie for over 25 years. I don't think I ever stopped loving her. And soon she'll be my bride, and I couldn't be happier with the thought.

But, something's bothering me.

Grandpa Abraham Weinberg was my favorite grownup when I was a kid. A Rabbi, he was never short on giving advice, but he did it in a way that made you feel better, not scolded. I think I was about 10 years old when Grandpa Abe sat me down for a talk.

"Bennie," Grandpa Abe said, "one of the reasons God put the Jews on earth was to do His worrying for Him. That's one of our jobs, Ben, to worry. I don't mean you should feel bad or unhappy, you just have to worry. It helps keep the world safe."

So, ever the obedient grandson, I'm worried.

Our country came within a filament of a disaster. Okay, we stopped it, but it was close. There are so many "what if's" that Grandpa Abe's advice will never get old, at least not for me. So okay, Grandpa Abe, Bennie's listening to you. I'm worried. Why?

Maggie provided the answer. While I sat in the den with my folks, Maggie was in the kitchen, listening to the radio and putting together some appetizers. She came running, not walking fast – running. Without saying a word, she grabbed the remote off the coffee table and clicked it at the TV.

"For those viewers who have just joined us, this is Shepard Smith reporting. Fox News has just learned that a nuclear suitcase bomb has been discovered in a van near the Parliament Building in London. Apparently the weapon has not yet been armed, and no timing device has been set. This news comes just days after a terrorist plot to set off nuclear bombs in five American cities was thwarted. Details are still coming in. We turn now to our affiliate in London..."

Bennie's listening, Grandpa.

THE END

WELCOME TO *THE GANG!*

The book you've just read, *A Time of Fear,* is Book Three of The Time Magnet Series.

The Gray Ship, Book One of the series, is a tale about an African American woman Navy Captain who, along with her nuclear guided missile cruiser, finds herself and her crew transported through time from 2013 to 1861, just before the start of the Civil War. "wildly entertaining, but also profoundly moving." Kirkus Reviews

The Thanksgiving Gang, Book Two of the series, finds Jack Thurber once again travelling through time, but this time into the future, where he learns that both he and his wife were killed in a terrorist attack. Jack has to go back to the past, to save his wife, as well as himself. "It's always nice to find a new voice in fiction and to enjoy creativity at its best."

You can find *The Gray Ship* and *The Thanksgiving Gang* on Kindle and paperback on amazon.com

I hope you enjoyed *A Time of Fear.* Please consider giving it a review on amazon.com.

Want to be updated on the next book in the series? Please copy this link and paste it in your browser to be added to my update list as well as a free subscription to my weekly blog on writing tips, *The Write Stuff.* http://www.morancom.com/

When you get to the site, just click on "Subscribe" and get updates in the right hand column.

ABOUT THE AUTHOR

I'm the author of *The Gray Ship* (Coddington Press 2013), book one of *The Time Magnet* series. It's a story of time travel, romance, and a nuclear warship that finds itself in the Civil War. *The Thanksgiving Gang* is the sequel, and *A Time of Fear* is Book Three in the series.

I have also published five nonfiction books: *Justice in America: How it Works—How it Fails.* (Coddington Press, 2011); *The APT Principle — The Business Plan That You Carry in Your Head.* (Coddington Press, 2012); *Boating Basics, the Boattalk Book of Boating Tips(* Coddington Press, 2013)*; How to Create More Time (*Coddington Press, 2014). I'm a lawyer and a veteran of the United States Navy. I live in Long Island, New York with my wife Lynda.

Made in the USA
Middletown, DE
23 September 2017